阿昌族非物质文化遗产丛书

英汉对照

阿昌族动物故事集

The Achang Collection of Animal Stories

杨叶生　成　功　编著
成　了（Selah Cheng）　译

知识产权出版社
全国百佳图书出版单位
—北京—

图书在版编目（CIP）数据

阿昌族动物故事集：汉文、英文/杨叶生，成功编著；成了（Selah Cheng）译. — 北京：知识产权出版社，2021.12

ISBN 978-7-5130-7858-0

Ⅰ. ①阿⋯ Ⅱ. ①杨⋯ ②成⋯ ③成⋯ Ⅲ. ①阿昌族—民间故事—作品集—中国—汉、英 Ⅳ. ①I277.3

中国版本图书馆 CIP 数据核字（2021）第 236549 号

责任编辑：高　超　　**责任校对**：谷　洋

封面设计：李　叶　　**责任印制**：刘译文

插图绘制：龙开元

阿昌族动物故事集（英汉对照）

杨叶生　成　功◎编著

成了（Selah Cheng）◎译

出版发行：	知识产权出版社有限责任公司	**网　　址**：	http：//www.ipph.cn
社　　址：	北京市海淀区气象路 50 号院	**邮　　编**：	100081
责编电话：	010-82000860 转 8383	**责编邮箱**：	morninghere@126.com
发行电话：	010-82000860 转 8101/8102	**发行传真**：	010-82000893/82005070/82000270
印　　刷：	天津嘉恒印务有限公司	**经　　销**：	新华书店、各大网上书店及相关专业书店
开　　本：	720mm × 1000mm　1/16	**印　　张**：	9.25
版　　次：	2021 年 12 月第 1 版	**印　　次**：	2021 年 12 月第 1 次印刷
字　　数：	200 千字	**定　　价**：	68.00 元

ISBN 978-7-5130-7858-0

编 委 会

生态环境部生物多样性调查、观测和评估项目（2019—2023年）
Project supported by the Biodiversity Investigation, Observation and Assessment Program of Ministry of Ecology and Environment of China (2019–2023)

阿昌族非物质文化遗产丛书

阿昌族是我国人口较少民族之一，主要分布在云南省德宏傣族景颇族自治州的梁河县和陇川县。阿昌族具有自成一体的传统文化与生活方式，但是目前仍然没有得到足够的重视，也缺乏必要的保护。为此，本丛书尝试将阿昌族的既有研究与未来发展纳入公众视野之中，力争呈现阿昌族传统文化的方方面面，为保护文化多样性，促进阿昌族社会生态系统可持续发展，略尽绵薄之力。

阿昌族非物质文化遗产丛书

总序

序言应该简短，不宜喧宾夺主。一套丛书的总序，更是应该克制，好像路边的指示牌即可。

现代社会有一个迷思，仿佛不同的社会和文化，不过是同样的现代人在不同的自然地理环境中的适应现象。如果把不同社会中的人放在一个具体的时空范畴内，他们就会复原为基本的样式，从而表现出一种混合的文化现象。

基于上述想象，人类获得了某种平等与一致性，而这既有着自然科学上生物学的分类学支撑，还为现代社会的文明提供了“不言自明”的基本框架。

这样的信念，引导着人们确信现代意义上的“人同此心，心同此理”，并将之作为全球化的奠基石。为此，在表面上尊重不同文化的表象之下，潜伏着某种解构一切文化差异的野心。

这套丛书希望发出一丝微弱的声音，提醒读者意识到文化多样性比我们的想当然要深刻复杂得多，跨文化交流和跨物种交配一样，很容易产生不马不虎的马马虎虎。有两个基本的解决方案可以化解这样的尴尬。

其一是重生方案，就是一个人可以在一个社区里出生，具有这个文化的内部视角，然后机缘巧合，他在另外一个社区里得以重生，获得新社区的文化身份和认同。比如一个孩子，出生在中国的洛阳，10 岁开始在澳大利亚的墨尔本人家里借宿读书，他有可能拥有完整的中国认同，也有全面的澳大利亚惯习。

这其实是人类学家梦寐以求的获得社区新身份的过程，虽然大多数人类学者内心很早就放弃了这种努力，毕竟，人已经老了，如何能重生呢？岂能再进母腹生出来吗？

另外一个是退而求其次的同情性理解方案。这需要先承认自身已经很难获得真实的异文化身份与认同（更遑论从来没有存在过的纯粹不杂），那么不妨接受这现实，然后怀有克制的好奇心和善意的同情心来理解异文化，进而可以具有对于自身固有文化的审视能力和批评精神，跳出自以为是的狭隘视野，不再做井底之蛙。这方案的侧重点在于对自身的反思和批判，“他山之石可以攻玉”。

本丛书就是希望读者获得后者的助益。孔子曰：“益者三友，友直，友谅，友多闻，益矣。”以不同的声音，提醒自己世界很大，价值很多，人生很短。

阿昌族是一个人口很少的民族，大部分生活在云南省德宏傣族景颇族自治州。但是这个民族并不小，因为他们具有自成一体的文化，在他们的世界里，有宇宙创造的图景，有社会运行的途径，有人类生存的价值。所以不能用小来形容这样的一个民族。

遗憾的是，阿昌族的传统文化正如同江河东流一样逝去，年轻的一代人无意传承古老的歌曲，更无法相信古老的信仰。等到某一天，他们不再年少，纵然意识到非物质文化遗产的价值，也可能为之晚矣。

现在，我们想做一些力所能及的工作，记录下某些东西，给出我们的声音，让一种文化不至湮没无音。同时，也请我们的读者不要用学术的冷漠来阅读，不妨用孩子的耳朵去聆听。

如果不是有一些不得不说的话，实际上大可不必有这篇序。

丛书总编：成功
中央民族大学生命与环境科学学院

Achang Intangible Cultural Heritage Series Preface

Foreword should be brief and serve the content of the book. A preface to a series of books should be as concise as a roadside signpost should.

There is a myth or misconception or an assumption in modern society, which holds that different societies and cultures are nothing more than what would come about when modern people adapt to a physical environment they are relocated to. In other words, if people in different societies were placed in a specific time and space, it would restore the norms of that environment, hence present a mixed cultural phenomenon.

Based on this assumption, humans have achieved certain sense of equality and uniformity, which is supported by the biological taxonomy of the natural sciences and provides a “self-evident” basic framework for civilization in modern societies.

Such a belief leads to the conviction of the modern expression (term) that “all men have the same minds and the minds follow the same reasoning”. Furthermore, it is considered the cornerstone of globalization. Beneath the polite facade of respect of different cultures lurks an ambition to deconstruct all cultural differences.

This series of books hopes to make a faint sound against what is taken for granted, reminding readers that cultural diversity is much deeper and more complex, and that cross-cultural communication, like cross-species breeding, is prone to produce something that is neither fish nor fowl. To avoid such an awkward result, there are two basic solutions.

One is the rebirth solution, in which case a person can be born into one community and develops an internal perspective of that culture. Then, by chance, he is born again in another community, acquiring the cultural identity and recognition of the new community. For example, a boy was born in Luoyang, China, and at the age of 10, he started to live and study with a Melbourne family in Australia. The boy might have a full Chinese identity and a full experience of Australian way of living.

This is an anthropologist's dream process of acquiring a new identity in a community, although most anthropologists had given up on this endeavor long before. After all, "How can someone be born when they are old? Surely they cannot enter a second time into their mother's womb to be born".

Another way is to settle for the second best option of empathetic understanding. It is necessary to see that it is hard enough to obtain one's own identity and identification with a different culture, not to mention genuine identity and identification of a different culture, which is technically non-existent. We may as well accept the fact and understand alien cultures with restrained curiosity and well-intended compassion, which then helps us to reflect upon and criticize our own inherent culture, leave our narrow-mindedness behind and embrace a broader view on different cultures. The emphasis of this project is on self-reflection and criticism, so to speak, "other stones can be used to carve jade".

It is the benefit of the latter for the readers that serves as the purpose of this series of books. Confucius said, "Three kinds of friends are beneficial to a person—friends who are straightforward, friends who are sincere, and friends who are knowledgeable." Amidst so many different voices, we remind ourselves that the world is vast, values are various, and life is short.

The Achang people are a very small group. The majority of them live in the Dehong Dai Jingpo Autonomous Prefecture Yunnan Province. But these people are not insignificant, because they have a self-contained culture, and in their world, there is a picture of the creation of the universe, a way of running society, and the value of human existence. The word "small" doesn't do justice to such an ethnic group.

Unfortunately, the traditional culture of the Achang people has paled into the background or faded with time. The younger generation has no intention of passing down the old songs, nor can they observe the faith of the old people. Perhaps one day when they are no longer young, they will realize the value of intangible cultural heritage, but it will be too late.

At present, we want to do what we can to record all that matters and make our voice heard in hope that this ethnic culture won't be lost without even being known to the world. At the same time, we invite our readers not to read like an indifferent academic, but to listen like an attentive child.

This preface wouldn't have been necessary if there were not anything that had to be said.

Editor-in-Chief
Dr. Gong Cheng
College of Life and Environment Sciences
Minzu University of China

前　言

阿昌族动物故事集的来由

在我们收集阿昌族故事的时候，我们最初没有意识到这些故事对于他们是怎样的一种叙事，而是将其看作我们给儿童讲的睡前读物，不过是一种消磨时间的趣味。

但是，当我们开始逐步分析他们的世界，理解他们的言行的时候，才发现，这些故事与其说是娱乐的，不如说是解释性的。因为他们用这些故事来解释他们生活中的事件。比如，亲姑太和后姑太的故事，不仅富于对照，而且解释了当地的血缘社会。同时，许多故事又是其中重要的习俗和节日的依据。

于是，我们开始了故事的收集和整理。这次，不同于传统的民俗学调查，我们不仅重视故事的文本，更希望关注故事的阐述和建构。

然而，一个新的问题出现了。我们作为跨文化的人，已经进入了某种内部视角，因此不知不觉学会了阿昌族的看法，因而失去了外部性。更可能的是，我们的理解，是一种不伦不类的认识。这种认识既可以被当地的人勉强接受，也可以被外乡的人心领神会，但它已经不具备这个故事本来可以表现的张力了。这需要借助不同社区里不同文化群体对于同一个故事的感受和教训并列出来，呈现出故事的多义性和文化的多样性。

所以，我们必须想办法获取进入田野的那种讶异感，并且能够把这种张力呈现给我们的读者，让读者不至于被翻译成汉语或者英语的文本带入自身文化的前理解之中。

我在阅读《伊索寓言》的时候，感受到了这种跨文化的张力。在每一篇《伊索寓言》的后面，都有一个解释。但是这个解释经常不能有助于我的理解，反而把我的理解搞得没有自信了。举两个例子：

驴和青蛙

有头驴驮着木料过沼泽地，脚下一滑，摔倒了，起不来，直哭。沼泽地里的青蛙听见驴哭，说道：“喂，朋友，你摔一下就这样痛哭；像我们这样在此长住，又将怎样呢？”

这故事适用于一种庸庸碌碌的人，这种人能够忍耐大的困苦，对于小的挫折却难以承受。

蛇和蟹

蛇和蟹同住在一个地方。蟹对蛇很直率、善良，蛇却总是那么阴险、邪恶。蟹一再劝蛇对他也要直率点，要学他那样为人。蛇就是不听。蟹很生气，趁蛇睡着了，夹住他的喉咙，把他掐死了。蟹见蛇直挺挺地躺在那里，就对他说：“朋友，你现在死了，用不着直率了，可是我劝你的时候，你却不听。”

这故事宜于讲给那些生前对朋友干了坏事、却要在死后留下善言的人听。

如果我把我们的理解，以及当地人的理解，作为伊索寓言的“教训”，就可能产生一种原来如此的理解，以及为何如此的理解。跨文化的对话才能彰显出这种“不同”。这是读懂他者的跨文化之旅。正好我所处之境具备了跨文化阅读的可能性。

我打算找一些 10 岁左右，母语是阿昌族语言的孩子，让他们听阿昌族老人用当地的阿昌语讲这些故事，并且问他们听了之后，有什么感受和想法，得到什么教训和道理。这样的结论，可以作为阿昌族文化内部自生的理解。当然，也需要采访这个故事原初的讲述者，他在讲这个故事，是希望提供怎样的说理。

然后再找一些北京的孩子，也是 10 岁左右，可以清楚明白地表述自己的想法和意见。让他们听我讲这些故事，然后询问他们的心得和体会，这些道理怎么样。这样的结论，可以作为阿昌族文化外部衍生的理解。北京孩子的理解，很可能反映出系统的学校教育的效果和理念。

这两种文化之间，有没有张力？或者这些不同，是来自取样的误差？这些都是难以解决的问题。哪怕增加样本量，解决的可能性也非常有限。而且我对于定量研究，特别是这种文化研究上的定量，保持某种克制。

所以，我又设计增加了一个对照组。这个人群来自美国一个很传统和普通的社区小学。为了让孩子更容易理解，我采用了口译的方式。就是我来先讲一遍，然后逐字逐句让孩子进行英译，并用视频记录下来。之后进行文字整理，再让孩子老师讲给她的学生听。之所以不让孩子来讲，是担心孩子在讲故事的时候，用太多的非语言的信息。然后，请老师记录孩子们的不同理解。在征得孩子的监护人同意的情况下，把这些反馈作为对故事的理解，也记载在故事之后。

这种方法，借鉴了经典对读的方法和理论。经典对读是寻找一个话题，在不同的宗教经典中，找到对应的论述，并且由信仰群体内部的人员进行阐述。这虽然可以避免那种隔靴搔痒，但是也会部分地带来理解的障碍。而这种障碍本身也成为一种跨越的挑战。民间故事的跨文化阐释，可以在成年人中进行。不过，似乎成年人在表达的时候，更加注意某种正确性，这种正确性需要更专业的解读。

这样的研究方法出发点认为，对于同一个故事，不同的文化会有不同的立场和态度（甚至同一文化的不同群体），因此可以凭借不同的感受，表现文化的差异，从而理解世界的文化多样性。

遗憾的是，做这样的探索需要大量的时间和精力，而我两者都不具备，所以暂付阙如。不过我仍然把这个设计记录下来，方便其他人如果有这样的条件，不妨尝试一下这种方法。

目前这本《阿昌族动物故事集》只收录了 31 个故事，都是杨叶生先生精心挑选的，能够较好地代表阿昌族的口头故事传统。

我们根据这些年在阿昌族地区的田野工作经验和感受，给每个故事写了一个编者按，希望可以把我们的观察作为故事的一种阐释，方便读者意识到故事的多义性和文化的多样性。

成了（Selah Cheng）在过去的两年里，三易其稿，完成了这部分动物故事的英译。虽然不会尽善尽美，不过应该还留有一个孩子的口吻和趣味，希望比严肃的英文更能够得到故事的神韵。

这些动物故事，是阿昌族讲给当地成人的，也是讲给孩子的。现在，是讲给大家的。

本书编者

于碧山居

2020 年 4 月 14 日

Preface

The Origin of the Achang Collection of Animal Stories

When we collected the Achang stories, we did not initially realize what kind of style of narrative they were for them, but rather saw these stories as nothing more than a fun way to pass the time, like the bedtime stories we tell children.

But as we gradually began to analyze their world and understood their words and actions, we realized that these stories are more explanatory than entertaining. For they use these stories to explain the events of their lives. For example, the stories of the real aunt and aunt by law are not only rich in contrasts, but also explain the local blood society or the basis for important customs and festivals therein.

So we began to collect and organize these stories. This time, unlike traditional folklore investigations, we wanted to focus not only on the text of the stories, but also on their elaboration and construction.

At the same time, a new problem emerged. We, as interculturalists, have entered into a certain internal perspective and have therefore unconsciously learned to view the Achang and thus lost our externalities. More likely, our understanding is something that is incoherent. It is something that can be grudgingly accepted by the locals or appreciated by the people in Beijing, but it is no longer the tension that the story could have presented. It needs to be juxtaposed with the feelings and lessons of different cultural groups in different communities about the same story, to show the multiplicity and cultural diversity of the story.

So, we have to find a way to get a sense of surprise into the field and to be able to present this tension to our readers so that they don't get caught up in the pre-understanding of their own culture with the text translated into Chinese or English.

I felt this cross-cultural tension when I read *Aesop's Fables*. At the end of each *Aesop's Fables*, there is an explanation, but this explanation often failed to help my understanding and instead made me less confident in my understanding. To give two examples.

The Donkey and the Frog

A donkey was carrying wood across the marsh, and his foot slipped, and he fell down, and could not get up, and cried. The frogs in the marsh heard the donkey crying, and said, "Hey, friend, you fall down and cry like this; what will you do if you live here as long as we do? What shall we do if we sojourn here as we do?

This story applies to a kind of mediocre person who can easily endure great hardships, but has a hard time tolerating small setbacks.

The Snake and the Crab

The snake and the crab live together in the same place. The crab was straightforward and kind to the snake, but the snake was always so sinister and evil. Crab repeatedly urged the snake to be straightforward with him and to behave like him. The snake just wouldn' t listen. Crab was so angry that he grabbed the snake by the throat and strangled him to death while he was sleeping. When the crab saw the snake lying upright, he said to him, "Friend, now that you are dead, you don' t need to be frank, but you didn' t listen to me when I told you to be frank. But when I advised you, you didn' t listen."

It is a good story to tell to those who have done evil to their friends in life, but want to leave good deeds behind them in death.

If I take our understanding, and the understanding of the locals, as the "lesson" of *Aesop's fables*, it is possible to create an understanding of what was so, and why it was so. It is only through intercultural dialogue that this "difference" becomes apparent. This is an intercultural journey to understand the other. I am surrounded by the possibility of intercultural reading.

I am going to find some native Achang children about 10 years old and let them listen to the stories told by Achang elders in the local Achang language and ask them what they feel and think, and what lessons and truths they have learned. Such a conclusion could serve as a homegrown understanding within the Achang culture. Of course, it is also necessary to interview the original teller of this story and what kind of reasoning he is hoping to provide in telling this story.

Then find some children in Beijing, also about 10 years old, who can clearly and understandably express their thoughts and opinions. Let them listen to these stories, and then ask them what they have learned and experienced, how these reasonings are. Such a conclusion can be an externally derived understanding of the Achang culture. The understanding of the Beijing children is likely to reflect the effects and philosophy of systematic schooling.

Whether there is tension between these two cultures, or whether these differences, from sampling error, are a difficult problem to solve. Even increasing the sample size has a very limited possibility of solving it. And myself maintain a certain restraint on quantitative research, especially on this kind of cultural research.

So, I've designed an additional control group. This population came from a very traditional and ordinary community elementary school in the United States of America. To make it easier for the children to understand, I used interpretation. This means that I will give the story first, and then the children do the English translation word by word and record it on video. After that, the children's teacher will speak to her classmates. The reason why I don't want the children to speak is because I am worried that the children will use too much non-verbal information when telling the story. Then, ask the teacher to record the children's different understandings of the story. With the permission of the children's guardians, this feedback is recorded as the understanding of the story and also after the story.

This method draws on the methods and theories of classical pair reading. Classical pair reading is the process of finding a topic, a corresponding discourse in a different religious classic, and having it expounded by someone from within the faith community. While this may avoid that kind of compartmentalization, it also partially introduces a barrier to understanding. And this barrier itself becomes a challenge to overcome. The cross-cultural interpretation of folktales can be done among adults. However, it seems that adults are more attentive to a certain kind of correctness in their expression, a correctness that requires a more professional interpretation.

The starting point for such an approach is the idea that different cultures will have different positions and attitudes towards the same story (or even different groups of the same culture), and therefore can express cultural differences by virtue of different feelings, and thus understand the cultural diversity of the world.

Unfortunately, it would take a lot of time and effort to do such a quest, and I have neither, so I'll leave it at that for now. However, I have recorded the design, so that someone, if they are in a position to do so, may try this method.

At present, there are only 31 stories in this *Collection of Achang Animal Stories*, which were carefully selected by Mr. Yesheng Yang to represent the oral storytelling tradition of the Achang people.

We have written an editor's note for each story based on our experience and feelings from our years of fieldwork in the Achang region. We hope to use our observations as an interpretation of the stories so that the reader will be aware of their multiplicity and cultural diversity.

Over the past two years, Selah (Le Cheng) has completed three drafts of the English translation of this part of the animal story. Although it will not be perfect, it should still have a child's tone and interest, and hopefully capture the spirit of the stories better than the strict English.

These animal stories are told by the Achang to adults and to children. Now, they are for everyone.

Editor
In Green Mountain
April 14, 2020

目录

动物是从哪里来的

据说很久以前，有一户人家住在大海边，家里有五口人，全靠打渔来维持生活。

孩子长到六七岁，父亲就带着三个孩子去求老师教他们读书。每天早晨太阳还没升上东山，他们弟兄三个就到了老师家等着。

有一天，他们弟兄三个正在跟着老师念书时，突然有一个长得很俊秀的小姑娘，轻轻地走进了他们弟兄三人的念书室，一声不响地听着老师教书。老师发觉后问她："你是哪家的姑娘？住在什么地方？"姑娘只摇头不答话，老师感到很奇怪。但是也不想更多地去盘问她，以为她是一个哑巴。

从那天起，这个小姑娘每天早晨都来，从未间断过。有时，弟兄三个还没到，她就先到了。老师再问，她还是不说话。

她天天来听课，一直到弟兄三个快要毕业时，她才开口告诉老师。

她说："我的家住在东海那边。老师，请你跟我去走一趟吧，到我家去逛逛。"老师问她："你家离这里远吗？"小姑娘说："我家离这里不远，一下子就走到了。"老师说："那好吧，就跟你去走一趟。"

说着，他们俩就起身到小姑娘家去。一路上，两人有说有笑，不觉来到了大海边。老师说："这么大的海隔着，又没有船。我两个怎么过得去。"小姑娘说："不要怕，过得去的，你跟着我走就是了，我走到哪里，你就跟着到哪里。"话才说完，她就牵着老师的手钻进了海里，一直到了海底，小姑娘的家就在这里。

他们俩到了小姑娘家后，小姑娘告诉老师：她是龙王家的大姑娘。她领着老师逛上逛下，一直逛了很多地方，不知不觉已来了七天了，老师想着要回去了。他对龙女说："我已来了好几天了，今天我要回家去了。"姑娘说："那好，我送你到人间去。"说完，她把送给老师的礼物包好后，就送着老师出了大海，到了海边。小姑娘对老师说："老师，这包礼物请你在半路上不要打开，等到了家后才能打开。"他们俩就在海边分手了。

老师背好了礼物包，就迈开步子走了。

走了一段路程，老师来到了半路上的一条水沟边休息。他想，这个小姑娘给我的这包礼物，如何这样秘密，说什么半路上不能打开，既然是礼物，在什么时候想看就得打开看。他就不管小姑娘说些什么了，想打开来看个究竟，到底里面有些什么贵重的礼品。

他把包包一打开，满包都是些动物，有各种各样的马、牛、羊、猪、鸡、狗、鱼、雀……还有一跳一跳的，乱跑的，他一下子顾不过来了。跳的跳，跑的跑。鱼跳进了水沟里，就在水里生活。老虎、豹子、老熊、兔子、麂子、马鹿等跑得快，一下子跑得很远，跑到了森林里，就在森林里生活。他赶紧把还跑不远的、跑不快的，很快抓回来包起，带回家里，等他到家再打开看时，剩下不多了。只剩下鸡、猪、鹅、鸭、猫、狗和马、牛、羊这些动物了，他就把这些关起来养，以后成了家禽、家畜，跑掉的那些动物都变成了野兽。

收集翻译：钱宝林

整理：钱宝林　张亚萍

编者按：这个故事开篇有一家五口，有三个孩子，但是这些细节在后文中无一呼应，让人初读费解。很多次听故事的人都会问，这些人怎么样了？因为在他们所听到的所有故事里，这样的伏笔都一定会有呼应。但是这故事里就是没有，因为这是一篇口头故事。口头故事的创作不同于书面创作，书面创作是高屋建瓴，纲举目张地建构。而口头故事的讲述，是被场景推动的，在线性的发展之中，只要故事还在继续，冗余的情节和人物都可以淡去。这好像是那种一镜到底的电影，不会分开交代多个线索。而在现实生活中，出现在一个人周边的事件，并不会紧密围绕一个故事发展，而是杂乱无章的。

Where Animals Come from

A legend was told a long time ago. There was a family of five people that lived in a house on the beach. There were three kids and their parents to be exact. They caught fish to survive.

When the kids were about six or seven years old, their father took them to a teacher to educate them. Before sun-rise, the three boys went to school on foot and arrived at the teacher's house and waited.

One day, when the brothers were studying, a lovely girl came into the room. She listened to what the teacher was saying without making any sound. The teacher asked her where she was from and lived. She said nothing. Though the teacher was confused, he didn't ask her more. He just thought that she couldn't talk.

From that day on, she showed up every day. Sometimes she was even earlier than the boys! The teacher asked her again. However, she said nothing.

She attended the class every day, until the boys were about to graduate. Only then did she start to talk.

She said, "I live by the east sea. Teacher, please come to my house with me for a short visit." The teacher asked, "Is it far away?" She said, "No, it's not far. Only several minutes' walk." The teacher agreed to go with her and said: "All right, I'll go with you."

While talking, they started to walk towards the east sea. On the way to her house they talked and laughed until they got there. The teacher commented, "The big sea is too big! There is also no boat to take us there." The girl answered, "Do not worry, we can make it. Just follow me wherever I go." As she was just done speaking, she held the teacher's hand and swam into the sea, until they reached the bottom of the sea, where her house was.

After arriving at her house, she told the teacher that she was the Dragon King's oldest daughter. She took the teacher to have a look at the house, going around every-where, inside and outside the house. Time went by so fast! They even didn't realize that seven days had passed when the teacher wanted to go home. The teacher told her that he had been there for a long time and he wanted to go home. She agreed. A few minutes later, she took the teacher to the land. She also gave the teacher a present. When they got to the shore, she told the teacher not open the present until the teacher got home. They separated at the shore.

The teacher took the present, and rushed away.

After a distance, the teacher rested on the side of a gutter. He thought about the present that the girl gave him: "Why is it so mysterious? Why not open it on my way home? Now that it is my present, I can open it whenever I want to." The teacher did not care much about what the girl said, he wanted to know what was in it.

When he opened the present, he found the whole present box was filled with animals. There were all kinds of horses, cattle, lambs, chickens, dogs, fishes, and lots more. There were also jumping and wild-running kinds. The teacher could not hold them all. Jumping kinds jumped and running kinds ran. The fish jumped into the gutter, so they lived in the water. Tigers, leopards, old bears, rabbits, deer and red deer all ran so fast that in a flash they went very far away, into the forest and lived there. The teacher ran as fast as he could to catch the animals that were not far and could not run very fast. He put them back into the present box and took them home. When he opened the present back home, there were not many animals left. Thc only animals left were chickens, pigs, Chinese geese, ducks, cats, dogs, horses, cattle and lambs, etc. The teacher reared them in pens, so they became domestic animals. While the runaway animals turned into what we called wild animals.

大象走路为什么轻轻的

“起卓勒混”猴在山洞生了小猴。多么可爱的小宝宝呀！它们半闭着眼睛，在妈妈面前翻筋斗，还“咿咿呀呀”地唱着歌哩！

忽然，山洞里唰唰地掉土。猴子急忙去查看。原来是大象从森林里闯出来，欢蹦乱跳，到湖边喝水，把山洞震动了。猴爸爸上前求告：“大象啊，请放轻脚步吧！下面就是我们的家。我们的儿女刚出世。你蹦蹦跳跳会踩塌我们的房屋，压伤我们的孩子。”

大象听了，把鼻子翘得老高，甩着尾巴，说：“爱蹦爱跳，是老子生就的脾气，你管得着吗？”

说完，它就迈开粗壮的肥腿，“咚咚”地小跑过去了，震得山洞顶部的土石唰唰地往下掉。猴妈妈和猴爸爸各自抱起两个孩子，三步两步纵出洞外。“轰！”——猴洞倒塌啦！

“起卓勒混”们哭啊哭。它们决心教训教训大象。

于是，它们从东山采来葛藤，又从西山砍来篾条。然后把山洞掘深，上面搭上几根竹棍，再盖上草皮。

第二天，大象又跑跳着奔来啦！猴爸爸又上去劝它放轻点脚步。大象不耐烦地叫起来：“滚开，黑猴！爱蹦爱跳是老象生来的脾气，改不了！”说完，它迈开大腿，一腿，一腿踏上草皮，只听“咕隆”一声，大象被陷进洞里啦！待大象摔醒时，“起卓勒混”们用葛藤和篾条把大象的四脚绑扎得结结实实的，一动也不能动，捆完，它们看了看，长叫一声，便到山林建筑新家去了。

大象被困在洞里，成群的牛虻飞来，叮在它摔破的皮肤上，饱吮一顿鲜美的血，把大象咬得浑身血淋淋的。太阳在头上烤，大象越发口渴、饥饿、疼痛。大象死命挣扎，挣脱一道篾箍，还有一道葛箍。这葛藤像牛筋样的牢固，大象已精疲力竭了。

大象不知睡了多久，它没精打采地睁开眼睛，瞟见月光下，黑猴在发笑呢！大象真想一脚踩死黑猴，无奈它的脚还被绑住。它听见黑猴问：“今后还敢乱蹦乱跳吗？”大象有气无力地摇摇头。黑猴又说：“改过就好！”说着，动手给它解去葛藤，捧给它几只山果。

大象感到不该莽撞，羞愧地低下了头。这以后，大象接受教训，走路放轻了脚步。它每天驮起黑猴一家到湖边去玩耍。“起卓勒混”们和大象成了好朋友啦！

讲述：藤茂芳

搜集整理：王国祥

编者按：阿昌族生活在中国和缅甸边境，大象曾经长期与阿昌族人们共同栖居一地，所以对于大象有切身的认识。这个故事利用了大象和猴子的体量差异，构成了一个冲突矛盾的背景。而猴子的聪明克制，大象的蛮横无理，颠倒了体格大小的优劣，让猴子获得胜利，让大象学习教训。以弱胜强，以聪明战胜蛮力，总是动物故事的要素，也是软弱而聪明的人类在动物世界的安身立命之所在。

Why Elephants Walk So Gently

A long time ago, some babies were born to a monkey family living in the cave. The babies were so adorable! While the baby monkeys couldn't even open their eyes, they flipped around in front of their mom. They even were "singing"!

Suddenly, the entrance of the cave started to rumble and crumble. The horrified monkeys looked around outside. Oh! It was caused by an elephant coming out of the woods, bouncing to get a drink by the pond. The father monkey implored, "Hey elephant, can you please walk gentler? Below here is my house. Our children were just born. If you keep jumping like that you will break our house and our children will get hurt."

On hearing this, the elephant put his nose up high and said: "I just love bouncing. It is my born nature. What does it have to do with you?"

After saying this, he trotted away, bouncing up and down. The underground house began to shake and crumble. The roof of the house came smashing down. The father monkey and the mother monkey held their two babies and flew out of the house. BANG! The house of the monkeys came tumbling down!

The monkeys wept and wept. They decided to teach the elephant a lesson.

At once, they got Kudzu (a climbing plant with long thin stems) from the east mountain and bamboo strips from the west mountain. They dug a very deep hole, put some bamboo sticks on the top and covered them with grass.

The next day, the elephant came trotting over again. The father monkey told him to walk gently, but the elephant was impatient. He called out, "Black monkey, I love bouncing. I was born with it. There is no way to change it!" After saying that, he started to bounce again. THUD! The elephant fell in the trap! When the elephant fell in, the monkey used the

Kudzu and bamboo strips to tie the elephant's legs up. He tied them so tightly that the elephant could not move at all. The mother monkey checked on him, laughed a little, then went off to build their house.

The elephant was trapped there, and pack of gadflies came and they drank the amazing blood from his body. In the hot morning light, he was thirsty, hungry and badly hurt. He tried to free himself, one Kudzu by one Kudzu, one strip by one strip. But Kudzu were so tight, he was exhausted.

The elephant slept and slept. When the elephant woke up, the moon was shining, and the monkey was laughing! The elephant wanted to kill the monkey with one step, but his feet were still tied up. He heard the monkey saying, "From now on do you still dare to always bounce like that?" The elephant was powerless, so he just shook his head. Then the monkey said, "Good for you!" Then he went down and untied the Kudzu, and gave the elephant some mountain fruits to eat.

The elephant felt that it should be ashamed of himself and embarrassedly lowered his head. After that, the elephant learned his lesson and walked gently. Ever after he picked up the monkey family every day to play by the lake. The monkey and the elephant became good friends forever after!

老熊为什么抓人脸皮

多少年以前，阿昌族居住的山上，不像现在这样光秃秃的。过去的山上，不但长满苍劲的油松、花桃，还有数不清的杂树，构成一片古老的原始森林。山上野兽很多，所以阿昌族关于动物的故事也就很多。例如“老熊为什么会抓人脸皮”就是其中的一个故事。

从前有兄妹两个，哥哥处处照顾妹妹，妹妹也很听哥哥的话。但是，哥哥是前娘生的，妹妹是后娘生的，前娘早死了，后娘是个偏心的人，经常虐待哥哥。她常想方设法地把哥哥打发出去做事，然后领着妹妹在家里做好东西吃。有一天，她又想了一个怪主意。她把兄妹两人找来，对他俩说：“春天来了，你们两兄妹上山去点豆子，各人点一块地，哪个的豆子不会出，哪个就上山守地，一直守到秋天收了豆子才行。”兄妹俩不敢反对，都同意了。夜里，后娘就趁兄妹俩睡着了的时候，把豆种分别装在两个背箩里，把其中的一箩豆种用铁锅炒熟了。

第二天一大早，后娘就叫兄妹俩上山点豆，她把炒过的豆种放在哥哥的背上，把没有炒过的豆种放在妹妹的背上，打发他们上山去了。哥哥走在前面，妹妹跟在后面，哥哥摸着自己的豆种热乎乎的，放在嘴里一吃，很香，就边走边吃。妹妹见哥哥吃东西，就问：“哥哥你吃什么？”哥哥回答说：“我抓豆种吃。”妹妹也抓自己背的豆种吃。觉得有一股生臭味，不好吃。哥哥说：“我的豆种很香，很好吃。”妹妹从哥哥的背箩里抓来一吃，确实很香，就要和哥哥换豆种。哥哥从来都是依着妹妹的，就和她换了豆种。

到了地里，哥哥先帮妹妹点豆子，妹妹又帮哥哥点豆子，种了三天才把两块地种完。过了三三得九天，后娘到地里一看，哥哥那块地的豆芽全长齐了，妹妹那块地里一棵也没有出。再过四六二十四天，妹妹的地里还是不出豆芽。后娘不好食言，只好在地头盖了一间窝铺，让妹妹去守豆子地。

有一天，妹妹坐在窝铺里撵雀，感到很孤独。突然，从箐沟里钻出一头老公熊来，它笑眯乐呵地朝窝铺走来，妹妹顿时吓昏了过去。当她醒来时，发现老熊还蹲在火塘边，不时地伸出舌头舔她的脚和手，而且它的态度温和，丝毫没有要伤害她的意思，从此以后，老熊就天天到窝铺里和妹妹玩，久而久之，妹妹和老熊建立了感情。

哥哥在家里种田，发现妹妹每天很晚才回家，而且神色越来越不对头，心里就产生了怀疑。问妹妹，妹妹红着脸什么都不说。有一天早上，哥哥执意把妹妹留在家里，自己一个人提把长刀守豆子地去了。中午的时候，哥哥正在地边砍树，老熊又像往常一样从箐沟里钻出来，笑呵呵地朝哥哥走来。哥哥一看，就明白了几分，他挥舞起长刀，把老熊杀了，在地边上挖了一个坑，把老熊砍成几节埋了。晚上，哥哥挎着长刀不声不响地回了家。

第二天早上，不等哥哥起床，妹妹就摸黑上山守豆子地去了。到了中午还不见老熊出来，妹妹非常思念，就到山头上望，山腰中看，山箐下瞧，路口上等。忽然，她在地边发现了一摊血，她沿着血迹找去，发现了一个新垒的土堆，连忙挖开来看。看到老熊被哥哥杀死了，她非常伤心，抱着老熊的头一直哭到天黑。哥哥在家里不见妹妹回来，就提着长刀上山去找妹妹，他在地边找到了妹妹，看到妹妹还在抱着老熊的头痛哭，他什么都明白了。哥哥知道妹妹已经做出见不得人的事，就用长刀把妹妹也……两只小熊突然从妹妹的肚子里爬出来，朝着深箐里跑去，他们边跑边说："舅爹，你杀了我们的阿爹和阿妈，以后你们进山里的时候，要把脸洗得白白的，我们碰上你们，就要抓你们的脸皮。"

从此以后，老熊就有了抓人脸皮的习惯。

搜集整理：杨叶生

编者按：这个故事很复杂，里面有几个话题，都是民间故事常有的要素。同父异母兄妹的设定，熟种子种地的情节，动物与女性的混血，埋伏杀戮的血腥，血迹寻亲的凄惨，兄妹相残的悲剧，这一切被熊会抓破人的脸皮给解释了。其实不是这个故事在解释为何熊会抓破人的脸皮，而是用熊的这个行为传说，来解释社会生活的禁忌与张力。这个故事很有口头特征，一直都是情节推动的，时刻充满了紧张和担心。最后，把对于森林遇熊的恐惧，与社会生活的禁忌联系在一起，会让听众有自己的价值判断和行为规范。

Why Bears Scratch People's Faces

A long time ago, the mountain where Achang people lived was not like nowadays. Nowadays there is barely any trees on the mountains. But long ago, on the mountains, there were not only pine trees, peach trees. There were also a lot of beautiful trees, and they together formed a wonderful primitive forest. On the mountains there were a lot of wild animals, so there are many interesting animal stories in the Achang town. For example, "Why bears scratch people's faces" is one of those stories.

Long ago, there was a brother and a sister. The older brother always took care of his little sister, and the little sister always obeyed the older brother. But the older brother was born to his father's first wife while the sister was born to his stepmother. His mother died. His stepmother was very biased on the little sister. So, she always abused the older brother. She always tried every possible way to make him run all errands, while she and the little sister made goodies to eat at home. One day, the stepmother thought of another wicked plan. She asked him and the little sister to plant beans in the spring, and told them they could not come home until the beans had grown up in the autumn. They were afraid to disobey. So, they agreed. At night, when the brother and sister fell alseep, the stepmother put seeds in two bags, and fried one bag of the soybean seeds in iron pan.

The next morning, the stepmother asked the brother and sister to go up to the mountain to plant the beans. She put real beans in the little sister's bag and put cooked beans in the brother's. The elder brother walked in front; the younger sister followed in the rear. When the older brother found out that the beans were really warm, he started to eat them. When the sister found out that the brother was eating, she asked him, "Brother, what are you eating?"He answered, "I am eating the bean seeds." She tried her seeds too, but they did not taste good. Brother said: "My beans are very fragrant, very delicious." So, she tried his beans and it tasted good so she asked to exchange her beans with the older brother. And he agreed, for he always yielded to his sister.

In the field, the brother and the sister planted beans. They helped each other. It took three days to plant the two plots. Nine days had passed. When the stepmother found out that the little sister's beans weren't growing, she knew that she had to keep her promise. Thus, she put a bed there and the little sister slept there.

One night, she sat in the bed driving away sparrows and she felt really lonely. When suddenly a bear came to her with a smile. She was really scared. She fainted away. When she woke up, she found the bear was still squatting by the fire and licking her feet and hands. She then realized that the bear meant her no harm. They soon became great friends. Since then, they had a relationship and even made love.

While the brother was farming at home, his younger sister came home late every day and the expression on her face was more and more unreasonable, and he was really suspicious about what had happened. He asked her what had happened when she was in the forest, but she gave no answer with a blush on her face. One morning, he told her to take a break and he would help to take care of the beans for her that day. Then he went out with a long sabre. In the afternoon, just when the brother was cutting a tree beside the field, the bear came happily as usual to the dating area. As soon as the brother saw the bear, he immediately knew what had happened to his sister. He waved his sabre in the air and killed the bear. After that, he buried the bear that had already been chopped into pieces. He went home that night very quietly.

The next dawn, when the brother was still sleeping, the sister went up to the mountain to watch over the bean field. Waiting until noon, the sister did not see the bear come. She missed him dearly, so she went all over the mountain to find him. Suddenly, she found a trail of blood. She followed that trail. There she found a new pile of soil. She dug it and found the bear! She cried and cried until it got dark. Not seeing his sister returning home, the brother was really worried. So, he picked up his sabre and went looking for her. When he found his sister crying and holding the bear's head, he instantly knew that his sister had done something shameful. He raised his sabre and killed his sister. Then he sliced open his sister's belly. There he found two little bear cubs in her belly. The little cubs ran away. When they were running, they cried, "Uncle, you killed our father and our mother. So, every time you human come into the mountains, wash your face clean. When we meet you, we will scratch your faces."

That was why bears started to scratch people's faces.

老虎为什么要咬人

传说古时候山林里并没有老虎，是后来才有的。老虎从哪儿来呢？阿昌族老人说下：老虎是由人变的。请听下面的故事，你就会明白了。

以前有甲、乙两个伙计，到很远的地方去谋生。他俩走到半路，盘缠用完了，前无村，后无店，肚子又饿，俩人就坐在路边歇脚。伙计甲觉得饿着不成事，总得找点吃的，便对伙计乙说："我变只老虎，去抬头野猪来吃。你看见我抬着野猪回来，就叫三声'伙计'，我就可以转复人身。然后我们一起烧野猪肉吃"。伙计乙还当伙计甲耍嘴弄舌，不以为然地说："咳！随你，变老虎，变乌龟王八都行"。

殊不知，说变就变，伙计甲在地上打个滚，眨眼工夫，竟变成了一只斑色大老虎，几蹿就蹽进箐棵去了。伙计乙看傻了眼，愣了好半天。待神志清醒后，伙计乙惶恐不安，浑身哆嗦，心想：他这样厉害，说不准什么时候会吃掉我。我千万不能和他在一起了。打定主意，他赶忙脱下身上的麻布衣，挂在歇气处的一棵小树上，自个儿爬到远处一棵大树上瞄着。

不久，老虎果然抬着一头野猪来了。来到原来休息的地方，放下野猪，绕着挂衣服的小树，抬头望着，转来转去；左望右望，听不到人喊它，老是转复不了人身。伙计乙看见了，连大气都不敢出。老虎转了几个圈子，还是听不见人叫它，便发了怒，震天动地地吼叫起来，加之饥饿难忍，用嘴撕开野猪，大口大口地吃起生肉来了。老虎吃饱后，看看挂衣服的小树，依然听不到人喊它，就拼命地扑上去，撞倒小树，把伙计乙的衣服撕个粉碎，气冲冲地走进山箐里去了。

伙计甲出门的时候，手上戴着一对镯头。变成老虎后，前脚上还留着一圈镯头样的花纹。从此，老虎和人结下了冤仇，见了人就要咬，见了人养的猪，就要抬去吃。

讲述：孙广诚

搜集整理：杨叶生

编者按：有史以来，人进虎退。老虎根本无法抵御人类的步步进攻，但是在人类开荒毁林的过程中，老虎是少数以伤人为反抗的动物。所以，老虎就成为某种威胁的象征，这种威胁从哪里来的呢？过去人不会用生态学的食物链来解释，他们需要一个更终极的答案，一个可以在人类社会的行为中有意义的答案。这样，人类之间的言而无信，以及受欺骗之后的冤屈就成为人与虎之间矛盾的解释。在现代社会，这样的故事很容易被受过教育的家长一笑置之，因为荒谬无意义。实际上，意义远非现代社会的这种平面的客观理性中立，意义可以是很立体的。让孩子，乃至成人，可以维持这个生动活泼的想象很有必要。

Why Tigers Bite People

Legend has it that there were no tigers in the forests at the beginning. They appeared afterwards. Then where did those tigers come from? The old people of Achang says, "Tigers are transformed from man." If you read the rest of the story, you will know what it means.

A long time ago, there were two good friends, Jia and Yi. They were going to a faraway place to work. When they were half way there, they had eaten up all of their food. There was no house in the front and no shop in the back, so they were very hungry. They decided to rest for a bit. Jia thought that without food they would not end well. So, Jia told Yi, "I am going to turn myself into a tiger, so I can bring a wild pig for us to roast. When you see me back with the pig, shout 'buddy' three times, then I will turn back into human. Then we can eat it." Yi thought that Jia had lost his mind, so he just replied, "Ok, whatever. You can change into a tiger; you could also change into turtle or else if you want."

Just like Jia said, he rolled on the floor, then in just one blink of an eye, he turned into a big tiger. All of a sudden, he leapt into the forest to look for food. Yi was stunned by what had just happened. It passed a long time before he knew what was happening. When he came back to his senses, he felt really scared. He started to shiver. He thought, "Wow! He is so merciless, who knows whether he will eat me off. No, I cannot stay with him!" With firm determination, he took off his shirt and hung it on the nearest tree where they rested. Then he himself climbed up a tree to see what would happen.

Not long the tiger did come back with a wild pig in its mouth. He returned to the place he rested, put down the pig and started to circle the tree that had the shirt on it. He looked up and down, right to left and circled it many times, but still he could not hear anybody calling him. Without a human's calling his name, he could not turn back into human form. When Yi saw this, he did not even breathe barely. The tiger circled it many more times, but still there was no one calling him. Jia got really angry. He started to roar. Plus, he had not eaten yet, so he swallowed the boar raw. When he was full, he looked at the shirt again. But still there was no one shouting to him. He pounced on the tree and made it fall, and ripped Yi's clothes to pieces. Then he stormed off from that place.

When Jia had left home, he wore a pair of bracelets with him. After turning into tiger, his front paw still had a bracelet-mark (strip-like) on his fur. From then on, tigers and men became enemies. Whenever tigers see a man, they bite him, and whenever they see a house pig, they eat it.

牛屎箍墩*

老虎凭着它力大气粗，在群兽中称王霸道。兔子虽然个儿小，却机灵聪明，要是比赛爬坡，谁也撵不过它。兔子在老虎面前，总爱装着乖巧的样子，然后想办法作弄老虎。所以，老虎把兔子恨透了骨，抓到兔子，总要把它坐得扁扁的，方才罢休。

不过，兔子戏弄老虎的事儿，也还是常常发生着。一天，兔子在一块草坪上，发现一泡大大的鲜牛屎。用这玩意，逗逗老虎，杀杀它的威风，也倒还有趣。兔子便用它前脚的利爪，削了一把竹签，然后插进牛屎里，乍看去签儿恰好不易被发现。兔子知道，老虎常来这里咬农人的牲畜，今天，让它受点教训吧！于是，兔子耐心地守在牛屎堆旁边。

不久，一只老虎，从树窠里钻出来，它扬着头，四处张望。看见有一只兔子坐在草坪上，便加快步子向兔子走来；双眼死死盯着兔子，嘴里的口水一滴一滴地掉下来。老虎担心兔子跑掉，便震天动地般怒吼了一声，想把兔胆吓破，好不费吹灰之力，就美餐一顿。可是，兔子早有防备，这一招已从同类的不幸中亲自领教过了。

老虎见兔子不为所动，出乎意料，十分惊疑，就问："喂！兔子，你在这里干什么？"

兔子回答得很干脆："守我老祖宗的箍墩。"

"嗬，什么箍墩，我坐一下"。

"咳！不行，我的老祖宗，个儿比你还大，知道了，会吞掉我，也会吃掉你。"

老虎听了，着实不服气："麂子野猪，哪样不是我的饭菜，有什么比我厉害的祖宗，你去叫它来！"

兔子听老虎的口气，知道它当真了，就做出一副恭恭敬敬的样子回答："好，你等着，我一定叫来"。

兔子一撒腿儿，朝着高高的山坡，顺溜溜地跑走了。

老虎围着牛屎堆转了一圈，见是软稀巴泥❶的样儿，于是翘起尾巴根，

---

* 箍墩：云南常见的用藤条竹篾编织的低矮坐凳。

❶ 软稀巴泥：方言，指像稀泥巴。

一屁股坐了下去。哪晓得，不坐还好，这一坐竹签统统戳进了老虎的屁股。老虎疼得龇牙咧嘴地叫个不停。兔子蹲在山坡上，远远看见老虎的狼狈相，禁不住蹦蹦跳跳地乐了一阵子。

搜集整理：杨叶生

编者按：兔子是谨慎弱小的，老虎是威风强大的。这种对立，让故事有了发生的空间。弱小的人物，不能用力量和强大的人物比较，他们选择了弱者的武器——诡诈。诡诈在一个传统农耕社会，并非现代商业社会这样可耻，反而是一种生存之道。弱小者以此在缝隙里生存，强大者默认弱小者以这种方式进行反抗，从而构成社会必要的平衡。因此，当一个现代的城市人进入传统的社区，想象着质朴无华的乡农，却遭遇了“愚穷弱私”（晏阳初语）的诡诈，经常有愤怒的感受。实际上，这是因为现代的城里人对于其他人的无知与傲慢，从来没有尝试去理解不同的社会文化。

Cow Poop Stool

Tigers use their strength and power to become kings of the forest animals. Rabbits are small, yet very clever. If they are going to race over mountain climbing, none can beat little rabbits. If a little rabbit meets a tiger, he likes to pretend that it looks obedient and cute. But in the end, it will try to play a trick on the tiger. So, tigers hate the rabbits very much. If a tiger catches a rabbit, he will always sit on the rabbit until the rabbit became flat.

But it happens pretty often as well that the rabbit tricks the tiger. One day, the rabbit was playing in a grass field and found a pile of fresh cow poop by accident. He thought that it would be really fun to use it to trick the tiger and puncture his arrogance. So, the rabbit sharpened a handful of bamboo sticks with his sharp claw on his front paw and then plugged them into the poop. At a glance, one can not see the sticks. The rabbit knew that the tiger often came to that place to prey on the farmers' livestock. "Today let the tiger learn some lesson!" So, the rabbit patiently waited for the tiger to come closer to the cow poop.

Soon, the tiger came out of the wood with his head lifted up and looked around. He immediately saw a rabbit sitting in the field. He quickened his pace to where the rabbit was sitting. The tiger stared at the rabbit, and drool fell from his mouth drop by drop. The tiger was worried that the rabbit would run away as soon as he saw him, so he roared as loud as he could to shake the world! He wanted to frighten the rabbit and breaking him into pieces. Then without any effort, he would be able to feast on the rabbit. But the rabbit was prepared for all of this, for the rabbit already saw what had happened to his friends when the tiger roared.

The tiger saw the rabbit did not even move, the tiger was a little unexpected and surprised, so the tiger asked, "Hey, rabbit, what are you doing here?"

The rabbit simply answered, “I am here to watch over my elder’s stool.”

“Oh, what stool! Let me sit on it.”

“No, this is my elder’s, also he is bigger than you. If he knows, he will swallow me and eat you! ”

The tiger heard this and did not give up. He said, “Deer or boar, which one was not my food? None can beat me in strength. Call your elder out! ”

The rabbit heard what the tiger said and knew that the tiger believed what he said. So, the rabbit pretended to respect the tiger and said, “Okay, please wait here. I will go and find my elder.”

The rabbit ran as fast as he could to the top of a mountain and instantly disappeared.

The tiger circled the cow poop once, seeing that it was just like wet mud. So, he raised his tail and sat on it. It would be better if he had not sat on it. The bunch of bamboo sticks all stabbed into his booty. The tiger was in so much pain that he shouted with agony. The rabbit was sitting on the top of a mountain and saw it very clearly. When he saw from afar that the tiger was in so much pain, the rabbit was so happy. He jumped up and down for a moment until he got tired.

豹子不咬水牛的由来

相传，豹子和小兔曾是好朋友。过去，豹子身上长着一尺多长的毛，灰绒绒的，既暖和又漂亮。为此，它常在好朋友兔子面前炫耀，并嘲笑兔子毛短。这让兔子心里越来越不自在，心想：一定要找机会整治一下豹子这个自大的家伙。

要整治豹子，对于弱小的兔子可不是件轻易的事。它想了好久，终于想到了整治豹子的妙计。一天，兔子约豹子一起盖房子。盖好房子后，兔子叫豹子上房顶，撒泡尿试试，看茅草屋顶漏不漏雨。豹子才爬上屋顶，兔子就在下面点燃茅草，把房子烘烘烧起来。豹子在屋顶见兔子跑得老远，转眼就不见了，自己身上的长毛正燃起来，晓得自己上了当，慌忙跳下房子，没命地乱跑。

豹子一边跑一边喊救命。跑了一截，遇到一匹马正在吃草，就喊：“马大哥，救救我。你瞧，我身上全是火。”马受惊时，常常会迎着风跑，于是它马上跟豹子说：“你迎着风跑吧，让风吹熄它。”豹子听了，就迎风跑去，结果身上的火被风吹得更大了。豹子一阵狂奔，遇到一头黄牛，又向黄牛求救。黄牛的性子，有事就钻草窠，因此它告诉豹子说：“往树林密的地方跑。”这下更糟，燃起来的草窠，把豹子烧得更惨。豹子慌忙钻出草窠，疯了一样地带着一团火乱跑。这时，它碰到一条水牛正在水塘里打滚。豹子带着哭腔，向水牛求救道：“水牛大哥，我要被火烧死了，快救救我吧。”水牛在水塘里动动身子，摇摇尾巴说：“快下塘来跟我打滚吧。”豹子听了，跳下水塘，打了几滚，身上的火全熄灭了。自己好不容易总算拣了条命，看看身上，灰绒绒的毛烧秃了，还留下一道道黄黑黄黑的斑纹，像镰刀一样。以后，人们把这斑纹叫作镰刀花。

从此，豹子恨透了兔子，一旦抓到就要把它当板凳坐扁；因为马和黄牛不给自己好点子，所以豹子一看见它们就会狠扑上去，咬死它们；只有水牛，豹子对它感恩戴德，从不咬水牛。

搜集整理：赵洪顺

编者按： 兔子并非君子，哪怕最后的结果是自己倒霉，还是忍不住捉弄那个总是让他嫉妒的豹子。对于强大者的嫉恨，是弱者的心理惯习。所以，如果对于别人总是不自觉羡慕忌妒恨，应该反思一下自身是否自卑和怯懦。动物的习性，在现代人眼中，需要的是生态学的答案，不过在传统社会，意义绝非那么遥远，而是在他们生活中日常经验到的各种心理。对于孩子，这些故事，哪怕不是那么光辉正确，但是可以让他们同情地理解。他们都知道这种捉弄人的报复快感。不让孩子经历这些，但将来还是会遭遇这些。经历并不等于会成为这样损人不利己的无赖，孩子需要从恶中见到光明。

Why Leopards Never Bite Buffalos

Legend has it that the leopard and rabbit have always been good friends. In the past, the leopard's fur was a few inches long and was of a grey color. It kept the body warm and was very pretty. Because of this, the leopard often showed off his fur in front of the rabbit and mocked the rabbit for his short fur. This made the rabbit really annoyed. He thought: I have to find a time to discipline this selfish leopard the arrogant guy.

It would not be a really easy task for the weak rabbit to teach the leopard a lesson. He thought for a long time until he came to an amazing idea. One day, the rabbit asked the leopard to come to build a house together. When the house was finished, the rabbit told the leopard to climb up to the roof of the house and pee there so as to see if the house had any leaks. As soon as the leopard climbed on the roof, the rabbit lit the thatch underneath and set it burning the house. The leopard on the roof saw the rabbit running away.In just a blink of an eye, the rabbit was gone. Meanwhile the long fur on his body began to burn. Then the leopard knew that he had been tricked. He imminently jumped off the house and ran for his life.

The leopard yelled as he ran. He ran for some distance and saw a horse eating grass, so he yelled out, "Mr. Horse, please help me! Look, I'm burning all over." When horses were frightened, they would run against the wind. So, he told the leopard, "Run against the wind, it will help you get rid of the fire." The leopard did as the horse said. But the fire got stronger when he did that. He had to run wildly again. Then he ran into an ox and asked for help. For oxen, when something happened they would get into haystacks. So, the ox told the leopard, "Go to the thickest part of the wood!" This time it was more horrible. The wood caught on fire. As the wood burned, the leopard himself was all on fire. He hurriedly ran out of the forest and found a buffalo rolling in a pool. He asked the buffalo for help, almost wailing, "Dear buffalo, please help me. I am going to burn to death." The buffalo waged his tail and invited, "Come down to the pool and splash in it. It will help you." The leopard understood and jumped in. It washed away the fire from his fur. And he was saved. But what was left of the fur was not grey, but yellow with black dots like a sickle. Later, people called this pattern the sickle flower.

From that day on, the leopard hated the rabbit. Every time he saw a rabbit he would sit on it. Every time he saw a horse or an ox (for not giving him a good idea) he would kill them. But every time he saw a buffalo he would be nice to him for he had helped him when he was in need. The leopard was always so grateful to the buffalo.

猴子是什么变的

大家常说："人是由猿猴变的。"可是在我们阿昌族群众中，却流传着一个很奇特的说法："猴子是人变的。"

相传在很久以前，由于遭受特大的天灾，人们的生活很困难。有一位寡妇，因男人意外死去，她一个人带着四个孩子生活。孩子最大的也只有五六岁，一家五口人面临着饿死的危险。于是这位妈妈把两个顶小的孩子抱到山里一棵结满果子的枇杷树下，让他们吃果子度日，打算等田地里有收成的时候再接回来。

年复一年，转眼就过了好几年。

有一年，老天照顾，这位妈妈种下一块水田，年终收成较好。粮食进家后，这位妈妈特意蒸了一大甑子雪白的新米饭，准备把两个在山里的孩子接回来。可这两个孩子已经习惯了森林里的生活，终年以吃果子为生，身体逐渐变了形，趋于野生动物，身上长出了很长的毛。

妈妈来到山林里接孩子。两个孩子听到妈妈的叫声，很想跑到妈妈怀里。但又很害羞，于是在很远很远的枇杷树上回答："妈妈，你回去吧，我们在这里生活行啦，我们身上长了很多长毛，已经不成人样了，回去小伙伴会笑我们，进寨子狗会咬我们的，织布、针线活也做不来了。"

妈妈听了孩子的话，痛心得一时不能自持，双手捂住脸，一股劲儿地往家里跑，不料从桥上跌下河里去了。

后来，两个孩子就变成了猴子，成了猴子的祖先。妈妈淹死在河里，变成了水里的蒙眼睛虫[1]。

搜集整理：曹连茂

---

[1] 蒙眼睛虫：一种水生昆虫，多在水田，身体小，中后足细长，两只前足粗短靠近头部便于取食，似蒙住头部。

编者按：不仅老虎是人变的，猴子也是人变的。人可以变化万物，而万物难以成人。因为人容易被“驯化”，按照人养，就是人样；按照猴养，就是猴样。这种能力被妥善利用，就是学习能力，人可以成为万物之灵，顶天立地；如果这种能力被强迫压制，就是驯化工具，人可以成为奴隶，变为野兽，寡廉鲜耻。万物不能进化成为人，但人很容易堕落成为兽。

Where Monkeys Come from

There is a saying: "Men evolved from monkeys." But in Achang there is a weird saying: "Monkeys evolved from men."

A long time ago, because of a great natural disaster everybody lived a hard life. There was a widow whose husband died unexpectedly. She had to raise up four children. The older children were six and five years old. When the whole family was starving, their mother brought the younger children under a loquat tree that was full of fruits. And she left them there to live on the fruits until the harvest in the field.

One by one, many years went by.

One year, thanks to the care of God, the mother planted a rice field, and had a good harvest. When the rice was brought back, the mother made a big pot of rice for the two children and went off to find them. But the children were already used to living in wild. They fed themselves on fruits. Their shape started to change and hair grew all over their bodies. They looked like wild animals.

Their mother went to the forest to pick them up. She called out to them.The children heard her and really wanted to run up to their mom and hug her. But they were ashamed of their appearance, so they said, "Mother, you can go back now. We will live right here in the forest. We grow hair all over and we are not like human beings anymore. If we go back, the fellows will laugh at us. Dogs in the stockade will bite us. Knitting and sewing are impossible now."

When their mother heard what they said, her heart was broken. She covered her face with her hands and ran home as fast as she could. However, she accidentally fell off the bridge she running on.

Later, the two children became monkeys, that is, ancestors of monkeys. Their mother drowned and became a midge in the water. [1]

---

[1] Midge: An aquatic invertebrate, mostly in paddy fields, with small body, slender thigh, and a pair of forearms covering the head.

兔子和豹子

有一只机灵的兔子，瞄到一窝马蜂，蜂房有一面铜锣那么大，兔子很想吃到蜂儿，但搔头挠耳，想不出点子。正在这个时候，一只豹子走来了。它看见兔子在那里，顿时抖起威风，冲着兔子说："今天，我饿得心慌打战，恰好碰着你了。"

兔子说："豹子大王，今天无论如何，你不能吃我。我在替官家守一个鼓。你要吃了我，官家是不会答应你的。"

豹子稍一掂量，也觉得官家兵多势大，惹恼了，招架不住。就松软了口气，对兔子说："那你守的鼓，可以让我敲一下吗？"

兔子说："你想敲鼓，要官家同意才行。"

豹子说："你赶快去问一下。不然，我要把你吃掉。"

兔子说："那你就等着吧。"

兔子跑到几十丈远的山坡上，站着回头对豹子说："官家同意了，要你闭着眼睛使劲敲三下。"

豹子刚闭上眼睛，兔子就悄悄逃走了。

豹子用前脚使劲敲打马蜂窝，由于用力过猛，一下子把蜂巢弄破了。千百只马蜂一齐飞出来，叮在豹子的身上。豹子痛得忍耐不住，睁开眼睛跑了九山十八坳，才摆脱了马蜂的追击。

豹子被马蜂叮得全身红肿，才发觉是被兔子捉弄了，非常气恼，心想，如果再遇着兔子，非把它吃掉不可。

一天兔子吃饱了食，蹲在一根青藤上，摇来荡去的，显得十分洒乐。这根青藤一头缠在树上，另一头挂在老树桩上，被打柴人砍了一刀，只是还没有断完。

不一会儿，豹子又恰巧来到了。他一眼瞧到兔子，真是冤家路窄。他气呼呼地对兔子说："前次你把我搞得好苦，今天终于碰上你了，这回咋个说，也放不过你了。"

兔子装着一本正经的样子回答说："今天皇帝派我守秋千，你把我吃了，等一下皇帝来荡秋千，你也休想活着回去。"

豹子听了，觉得暂时不吃也罢。但皇帝的秋千，我倒要试试，像皇帝一样快乐快乐。就对兔子说："你去请求皇帝，让我使一下皇帝的秋千，就再饶你一次。”

兔子说：“你要使秋千，我先去报告皇帝一声”。

豹子说：“你赶快去问，不然，我真的要把你吃掉。”

兔子转过身就赶紧跑了。跑了好长一段路，才回头对豹子说：“皇帝已经答应了，只能使三下，多了要处罚你。”

小兔说完，后脚一弹，跑了。

豹子站在青藤上，荡了一下，摇来摆去的，感到挺自在。又连荡了两次，更觉得舒服了。豹子想，反正兔子不在，皇帝也看不见，我不妨再荡一次。于是，豹子使劲一荡，藤子被挣断了。豹子被一骨碌甩到坳子底去了，腰骨也跌折了。豹子躺在那里，只能大声呼喊，却动弹不得。

这时，一只乌鸦飞来，落在树梢上，看见豹子躺在坳子底下，便笑开了。豹子勉强挣扎着抬起头，对乌鸦说：“乌鸦兄弟，请你救救我，往后有好吃的食物，一定忘不了你。”

乌鸦就飞到寨子里晒豆腐的人家，叼来豆腐皮，给豹子包腰骨。过了不久，豹子腰被乌鸦治好了。就这样，豹子得了一个“铜头铁尾豆腐腰”的绰号。豹子为了感谢乌鸦，就说：“以后，我咬死的牛马牲畜，吃剩的便让你吃。”

至今，凡是豹子吃过的东西，总是被乌鸦发现，乌鸦成群结队地飞去啄着吃。

搜集整理：杨叶生

编者按：兔子又一次戏弄了凶狠残忍的豹子。豹子显得非常热爱生活，想打鼓，想荡秋千，而且知恩图报，言而有信。兔子原本是豹子的食物，但是屡次用诡诈和诱惑，并借助了更有权势的官府话语。实际上大多数阿昌族老年村民都没有离开过本乡，对于他们来说，皇帝不过是一个权力的符号。不过，这个符号渗透到了动物故事之中，动物都学会了利用这种外来的，高于本土可见的有权有势的那伙人，遥远而神秘的权力来源。所以，这个故事并非简单地解释豹子的豆腐腰，也不是乌鸦为何总可以豹口谋食，而是解释了一个社会中力量的平衡，为常规的弱者在口头上建立某种力量。

Rabbit and Leopard

Once there was a clever rabbit; when he saw a big beehive, the size of a tam-gong, he really wanted to eat the honey in it. He thought for a long time, but could not get any good idea. At that time, a leopard walked by. As the leopard saw the rabbit, he spoke in a kingly way: "Today, I am really hungry and now I see you."

Rabbit replied: "King leopard, you cannot eat me today. For I am guarding a drum for my master. If you eat me, my master will not be pleased."

The leopard thought that the master was really in high power. If he did anything wrong and made the master mad, it would not be good. He let out a long sigh and then said: "Can I drum the drum you are guarding?"

Rabbit answered: "If you want to drum it I have to ask permission of my master."

The leopard replied: "Go and ask quickly or I will eat you!"

Then rabbit said: "Fine, wait here please."

Rabbit ran a mile away then turned back to the leopard and shouted: "The master agreed, and you can drum it three times with your eyes closed."

When the leopard closed his eyes, the rabbit had already disappeared.

The leopard used the front paws to hit the drum (which was a beehive), but he hit it too hard that made a crack in it. Hundreds of bees came out. They burst out to sting the leopard. The leopard could not bear it anymore. He opened his eyes and ran for his life. He ran for a long time until he finally got rid of the bees.

The leopard was stung all over. He knew he had been tricked by the rabbit. The leopard was really be annoyed, and he thought that if he saw the rabbit once again he would eat him no matter what might take.

One day, when the rabbit was full, he sat on a vine and swung back and forth. He looked very happy. Coincidently, One end of the vine was on a tree; the other end was on a tall stump of a tree. The vine was slashed by a wood cutter. It was almost going to fall but not yet.

Coincidently, as the rabbit started play, the leopard came around. When he saw the rabbit, he became very angry and said in a mean way: "Last time you almost killed me. Now I finally meet you. You can say whatever you want, but this time I will eat you no matter what happens."

The rabbit pretended to be seriously answer: "Today I am guarding for the king's swing. If you eat me you will not come out alive when the king comes here to swing."

The leopard heard this and thought that it would be alright not to eat the rabbit now. But the king's swing, he wanted to have a try. Being as happy as the king would be amazing. Then he said to the rabbit: "Go and ask the king if I can swing on his swing, then I will spare you again."

The rabbit said: "If you want to swing I will ask the king."

The leopard replied: "Ask quickly or I will eat you for real."

The rabbit turned around and ran away fast. He ran for a long time then he turned around and said to the leopard: "The king agrees to let you swing, but only for three times. If you swing more you will be punished."

While saying this, the rabbit bounced with his back legs and jumped away.

The leopard stood on the vine and swung once. It swayed around and around. He felt great. He swung two more times and felt comfortable. The leopard thought that since the rabbit was gone and the king could not see, why not swing a few more times? So, the leopard did. But when the leopard swung one more time the vine snapped. And the leopard fell to the pit underneath it. The leopard's waist bones fractured. The leopard lay there. He could not move but only yelled.

At that time, a raven flew past and landed on the tree. When he saw the leopard lying there, he burst out laughing. The leopard raised his head slowly and said to the raven: "Raven brother, please help me. If I find something good, I will never forget you."

The raven flew into a tribe and brought back some dried tofu from people's houses and put them on the leopard's spine. Not long after, the leopard's spine was cured by the raven. And that is why the leopard's nickname is "a hard head and tail but tofu spine". The leopard was very grateful to the raven and said: “When I kill a cow or a horse or something like that, whatever food I don’t eat, it will be for you guys’.”

Up to now, whatever the leopard eats left, the ravens will be the first one to find it for food.

水牛没有上牙的由来

从前，有一头水牛，被人驾着千筋弯担犁田。将近中午，牛已经疲倦，拖起犁来很吃力，时不时还要挨上两撇索。有一只豹子从箐棵跑出来，瞧见水牛拉着犁慢慢地在田里走，就蹲在田埂上看。豹子觉得水牛太老实，便对水牛说："你这样乖，把千筋弯担拉烂，跑掉嘛。"水牛听了回答说："人的主意高呢，我们搞不赢人。"

豹子听了，感到很好笑：山中我为王，世上的人能有多高的主意。便向人问道："你的主意多高，让我看看。"人笑笑说："我的主意可高了，只是这下放在窝棚里。"豹子说："你拿来给我看看。"人说："要拿，可以！不过你要让我拴着。"豹子说："不用拴。"人说："不拴，你会跑掉。落得我白跑一趟。"豹子听了，说："照这样说，你就来拴吧。"人卸下千筋弯担，解下撇索，把水牛放去啃草。然后，把豹子的四条腿捆住，拿起水打脚[1]就敲。水牛坐在田埂上，看见豹子挨打，张着嘴乐得合不拢，由于埂子窄，水牛一不小心跌到埂下，上嘴碰在石头上，把上牙磕掉了，所以，水牛至今没有上牙。

人把豹子痛打了一顿后，解开撇索把它放走了。豹子被打得筋酥骨软，十分气恼，一边跑一边发誓："我要一年下十二窝，吃绝人哥哥。"由于仓皇逃窜，冷不防撞着一棵青冈栎树，惊动了在树上乘凉的利柴鸡。利柴鸡普噜噜叫着飞起来。豹子碰得头昏眼花，把利柴鸡叫的声音听成人在喊"短着"[2]，吓得三魂七魄不附体，以为人已经飞到面前来收拾它了，急忙改口说："我十二年下一窝，活的少，死的多。"怕人不相信它，还保证说："人哥哥路上走着咳一声，我听着绕道走。"

所以，在我们山间路上行走，只要有咳嗽声，豹子就不会迎面走来。

记录整理：杨叶生

---

❶ 水打脚：犁具的组成部分，套在耕牛后腿上。

❷ 短着：挡住路口。

编者按： 豹子一如既往地狂妄自大，也毫不意外地被教训了一顿。这次戏弄豹子的，不是兔子，而是人类，虽然这个人用的方式和兔子差不多。作为奴才的水牛，不仅认了命，而且还幸灾乐祸地把自己的上门牙摔光了。这是一个被奴役的生物，不仅自身挨揍，还乐于看到自由自在的豹子被痛打。而豹子在被人教训之后，原本叫嚣得很，想在口头上占便宜，却因为听到风声鹤唳的声音，马上改口认怂，求饶保命。这样，水牛才能继续安心做水牛，因为离开了有权有势的人类，也混得很悲催。

Why Does the Buffalo Have No Upper Teeth

Once there was a buffalo. It was led by people to farm. When it was near the noon, the buffalo was tired out. It was really hard to plow. Sometimes the buffalo might get hit. A leopard came out of the woods and saw the buffalo plowing slowly. He sat down and watched. The leopard thought that the buffalo was too obedient, so he said to the buffalo "You're so obedient. Why not break the rope and run away?" But the buffalo answered, "Humans have better ideas than ours. We cannot beat them."

The leopard heard that and began to laugh, even feeling amused, "I am the king of this forest, no one has a better idea than mine." Then he asked the man, "if you have a better idea then let's see it." The man smiled, "My ideas are brilliant, but I have left them in the shed." The leopard answered, "Go and get them for me." The man said, "I can go and get them, but I will have to bind you." The leopard said, "You do not need to bind me." The human answered: "If I do not bind you, you'll run away. Then I will have nothing." The leopard heard it and said, "Fine, in that case you can bind me." The man brought down a very strong rope from the buffalo's mouth and let the buffalo eat the grass. Then the man bound the leopard's four paws, picked up a wooden club and began to hit the leopard. The buffalo, watching the leopard being hit, laughed so hard that he could barely close his mouth. Because the stump was thin and small, the buffalo fell off and knocked out his two upper teeth. So, the buffalo has no upper teeth.

The Human hit the leopard for a long time, loosened the rope and let him run away. The leopard was sore all over and very angry. He said while running, "I will have twelve cubs in one year and eat all the human beings." Because the leopard ran too fast for hide, he hit a tree. The birds in that tree were frightened by the sound. Then the birds all chirped. The leopard was dizzy and thought, the chirping was the man calling "wait".

He was scared and thought, the man had already ahead of him, and changed his words: “I will have one cub in twelve years; only a few will live.” He was afraid that the human would not believe him, and he also promised, “If a human fellow coughs, I will not come to thee. I will go the other way.”

So, every time when we are walking in mountains, we just need to cough a bit then the leopard will not come to us.

水牛恨老龙

相传很早以前，水牛和人一样会说话。耕田犁地，农人都要和水牛商量，水牛同意了，才能驾犁干活。

有个农人，养着一头水牛，每到下田的时候，它就推三拖四，不愿出力。主人和它商量说：“你该下田做活了。”它总是扯野：“我没有力气，等过几天再说吧。”农人眼看小满节已过，别人的苗棵开始转青，自己的秧还插不下，真是心急火燎。一天，有条老龙从虚空看到有片水田荒着，便腾云驾雾，飞来巡察。老龙见农人荷锄叹息，愁眉不展，便问：“你的田为何不栽不插？”农人回答：“我那头牛懒病发，左催右催，就是不愿干活。”老龙听了，捋着髯须哈哈大笑起来。农人见老龙发笑，丈二和尚摸不着头脑。老龙察觉，农人憨厚老实，没有主见，便给他出了个主意。老龙说：“水牛不想下田，是它怕出力，只要吃烟的时候，用燃着的火草在它的下嘴壳底面灸一次，力气就会大起来了。它再不动，你就用撇索吆。”农人照老龙的话，在指定的部位灸了一次。水牛果然像吃了哑泉水一样，再也不会说话了，灸过的地方，生起了一个蚕豆大的包块。

第二天，农人叫水牛下田，水牛扬着头，一声不吭。农人又照老龙的话，理起了撇索。水牛见人要用绳子打它，就赶紧下田去了。农人一边犁田，一边自言自语：“真让老龙说对了。”水牛听了只会张口，却说不出话来。

从此以后，谁家的水牛不想下田，主人就照这个农人的做法，在水牛的下嘴壳底面灸上一次。户传村，村传寨，人们用这个办法，把水牛全部灸哑了。水牛终于恍然大悟，知道上了老龙的当，不但再不能说话，还要挨主人绳索的鞭打。水牛恨死老龙，互相邀约串通，要向老龙报仇。所以，遇着烂泥塘，水牛都认为有老龙住着，要走去打滚，拉屎拉尿，把泥塘弄脏，再用双角使劲地拱稀泥，好让老龙上不了天。

至今，水牛下嘴壳底面仍有一个疙瘩，传说就是农人用火草灸了后，遗留下来的烙印。

讲述：杨叶盛

搜集整理：孙加申

编者按：到底是谁在奴役鞭打水牛？是谁在火炙烟熏牛的下嘴壳？是人类。但是水牛似乎并不仇恨人类，反而对于那个出馊主意的龙恨之入骨。实际上，水牛从来都没有亲眼看见龙给人出这个主意，水牛之所以相信是龙的坏点子，完全是因为人在用水牛犁地的时候，假模假样地自言自语“真让老龙说对了”。感觉这个故事完全是人类编造出来，嫁祸于龙，取利于牛。可怜的是水牛执迷不悟，反而祸害他们认为始作俑者的龙。这些水牛的手法也是毫无实效，不过是自欺欺人的阿 Q 做法。

The Buffalo Hates the Old Dragon

A long time ago, buffalos could talk just like we humans do. Because farmers needed buffalos to plow the dirt, they had to come to agreement of the deal first. When the buffalos agreed, they would go to plow the dirt.

There was a farmer who had a buffalo. Whenever go plowing the field, the buffalo always found many excuses for not laboring. The owner told the buffalo, “You are supposed to go and work.” The buffalo always answered, “I have no strength left, wait for a few more days.” The farmer waited until late May, when other’s fields have already turning green. But this farmer’s field was not plowed yet. The farmer’s heart was about to burst. One day, an old dragon looked down at the empty field and came down to check on it. The old dragon saw that the farmer was sighing and unhappy, then asked, “Why do you not plant your field?” The farmer answered, “My buffalo is really lazy. Even if I make it hurry, it’ll not move.” The old dragon heard that then combed his mustache and laughed. When the farmer saw this he got confused. For the old dragon saw that the farmer was honest and pure, he told the farmer a solution. The old dragon told him, “The buffalo does not want to go to the field because he is afraid to use strength. Only when he smokes, his strength will become stronger. Burn a blade of grass and use it to touch the buffalo’s lower lip. If he still does not move, use a whip to whip it.” The farmer did what the old dragon told him. The buffalo, as if he had drinken the water of silence, could not speak again. And where it was burned, it grew a little bump.

The next day, the farmer went down to get the buffalo.The buffalo raised his head and made no noise. The farmer again followed the old dragon’s instruction and raised the whip to whip the buffalo. The buffalo saw that the farmer was about to whip it, then quickly went to plow the field. The farmer, when farming, said to himself, “The old dragon was right.” The buffalo could only open his mouth but no words came out.

From then on, if someone’s buffalo did not obey to its owner, they would use the same way as this farmer, to burn the lower lip of the buffalo. By words of mouth, everyone used this idea. Now every buffalo was mute. The buffalo finally realized that he was tricked by the old dragon. So now they cannot talk, but also were whipped by their owners. The buffalo hated the old dragon. Whenever he saw a muddy place, he thought that the old dragon lived there. He would then roll in it, poop in it, and pee in it in order to make it dirty. What's more, he used his back legs to kick the dirty place so that the old dragon could not fly.

Even now, the buffalo still has a bump in his lower lip, and it is believed that it is the farmer who burned it.

九头牛精

很久以前，人们不兴杀牛。纵然牛老死了或跌死了，也任其腐烂，从不剥皮晒肉。总觉得牛为人苦累了一生，不应该吃它的肉，不忍心千刀万剐它。

有一回，一户阿昌族的一头大水牛摔死了，日光照着，变成了一头九个头的水牛妖精。九头牛精一夜要吃九个人的心脏。一到晚上，阿昌族人家就关门闭户，人心惶惶，哭天恸地。村寨中央，摆满了大鼎小鼎，香烟弥漫，男女老少三祈九叩，祷告上天为百姓除妖保佑。

玉帝耳烧眼跳，急忙派出太上老君出巡视察。太上老君来到南天门外，拨开云层，传下话来：

“尔等百姓为何痛哭流涕？”

“只因我们这一带出了个九头牛精，每天夜里都要来吃人心。”

“剥它的皮蒙鼓敲，剐它的肉晒干巴嘛！”

“它是吃人的牛精，我们捉拿不着。”

太上老君听罢，回禀了玉帝。玉帝赐给百姓一把寒光嗖嗖的宝刀。牛精一见宝刀，顷刻筋酥骨软，瘫倒在地。人们拧起宝刀，杀了九头牛精，将皮子蒙鼓敲，将肉切成小块，用竹竿串了晒干巴。

往后，一旦牛死了，人们就毫不留情地剐下它的肉，晒成了干巴。

讲述：杨叶盛

搜集整理：赵兴旺

编者按：杀牛还是宰牛？这是不同的。在传统的中原大地，私自宰杀耕牛是重罪，唐朝时候哪怕是宰自己家的牛也要判徒刑一年，在宋朝时候增加到了两年。因为在古代耕牛是核心的农业生产资料，是维持农业社会运行的重要基础，而且牛角和牛筋还是制作弓箭的材料，牛皮可以制作铠甲，这就是军事物资了。但是仍然无法禁止民间喜欢吃牛肉的爱好，特别是在水浒传里，英雄们都要两斤牛肉，这是一种挑衅官府的不羁行为。

另外一个吃牛肉的禁忌，来自社会的心理。牛往往和一个家庭生活得很紧密，好像家庭成员，而且吃的是草，出来的是奶，各种体力活都得干，长途运输，拉磨碾场，耕地开荒。一个如此任劳任怨的老牛，最后被杀了吃肉，于情于理总是过意不去的，特别是在一个人情天理的社会之中。那么，必须先把责任推卸到牛的头上，如果不吃牛，牛会如何如何。这样一来，宰牛吃肉不仅不是那么不近人情，反而是迫不得已的自卫，甚或是防患未然的练达。

这样说绝非含蓄批评讲故事的人虚伪狡诈。因为在这种阐释性的故事里，起码残留了某种不忍心，力图解释这种杀戮。而现代社会将牛直接安置在人类的食物链下，并且将宰杀隐蔽在视野之外的屠宰场，连一个有人情味的解释都不需要，就可以随心所欲地在超市中购买包装精美的牛肉。

Nine-Headed Cattle

A long time ago, people did not like to kill cattle. If a cattle died of old age or a fall, people left it rotting. People neither cut its skin nor ate the meat. They thought that the cattle worked for them until it died, so they did not want to eat its meat, or use a knife to cut off its skin.

Once, an Achang family's cattle died from a fall. Sun shined upon the dead body, and soon it became a nine-headed cattle monster. The nine-headed cattle always ate nine people's hearts at night. Deep at night, Achang families closed their doors tightly and were really scared. They even wailed and wailed. In the middle of the town there were many big and small tripods. With burning incense hung in the air, men and women prayed to the gods to protect them from this monster.

The Jade Emperor heard their pray and made Lord Taishang Laojun to look at the town. Lord Lao Zi went to the Southern Gate of the Heaven, cleared the clouds and asked, "Why do the people cry?"

"Because a nine-headed cattle was in our town. Every night it comes out to eat human's hearts."

"Then cut off its skin to pack a drum, and cut off its meat to dry off then!"

"It's a human-eating cattle monster, we cannot catch it."

Hearing this, Lord Lao Zi immediately reported to the Jade Emperor. The Jade Emperor gave the human a cold precious sword. When the nine-headed cattle saw the sword, it was really scared and fell to the ground. People took the sword and killed the nine-headed cattle. Then they cut off its skin to pack the drum and sliced its meat into small pieces and dried them on a bamboo stick.

From then on, when a cattle died, humans would not hesitate to cut off its meat and dry it off.

豹子坐猫

在远古的时候，豹子只会在地上行走捕食，不会爬树。有一天，豹子偷偷摸摸地来到寨子旁边拖猪吃，刚走到寨边的一块地里，看见一只老母猫领着几只小猫，在棕树脚下互相翻来覆去戏闹厮打着。豹子看了一会儿，见猫没有什么本事，就一步蹿跳过去扑老猫。机灵的老猫看见豹子扑来，就“儿呀”地叫了一声，一下子跳上了棕树，小猫听到妈妈的叫声，也都连忙溜上棕树去了。豹子扑了个空，气得不得了。它前抓后蹬，在棕树下转来转去，就是爬不上树去。老猫呢，蹲在棕树上，看着它一声不响。过了一会儿，豹子冷静下来，跪在棕树下向老猫乞求，说：“猫嫂，今天真对不起你，我打扰了你们。你们有这般非凡的本事，为什么不去捕鸟捉兽，而在这里互相打闹呀？”老猫话里有话地对豹子说：“我们学本领可不是为了伤害别人，而是为人大哥捉拿讨厌的老鼠。”狡诈的豹子顺势说：“那好！请猫嫂教我上树的本领，我也为人大哥去捉拿老鼠。”

老猫听到豹子也要为人大哥捉拿老鼠，有点心酸了。当年人大哥到西天接自己来的时候，只说在人间待三年，捉完老鼠就送回去。由于自己不小心，拿着的老鼠从嘴边逃走了一只，致使今天老鼠到处横行，自己不得回西天。想起这些，猫就答应说：“好，我教你。但有一个条件，学会了只许捉拿老鼠，不准伤害他人。”豹子为了学得猫的上树本领，然后吃掉猫，便答应了猫提出的条件。但老猫看到豹子还不够诚心，就只教豹子如何上树，而不教它如何下树。

豹子学了三天后，就想吃掉猫，又找不到借口，心中总是闷闷不乐。豹子的一举一动，老猫早觉察到了，它时刻都在提防豹子。这天，一只小花猫捉到一只老鼠，高高兴兴地给老猫送来。老猫从小花猫的嘴里把老鼠接过来，递给豹子吃。当老猫走近豹子时，豹子听到了猫的埋怨声，就对老猫说：“猫嫂，你的嗓子有一团棉花塞着，看你天天叽咕叽咕地好难受，我帮你挑掉。”说着，豹子张牙舞爪地朝老猫扑去。老猫“啊”的一声，就蹿上了棕树。豹子也蹿上去追，快上到丈把高的地方，老猫后脚一蹬，前爪一招，顺利地从棕树上溜下来，又蹿上一棵两丈高的棕树去了。豹子抓猫心切，也照老猫一样，后脚一蹬，前爪一招，往下溜，可是老猫没有教它这一招，结果从一丈高的棕树上跌下来，把腰骨也给跌折了。老猫为了给豹子尝尝自己的厉害，又从棕树上跳下来，用前爪抓了两把豹子的鼻子，把豹子的鼻子抓出了血。摔伤了身子的豹子被抓得动弹不得，幸亏被一只黑乌鸦看见了，豹子向乌鸦苦苦哀求，乌鸦就飞到农人的田房窝铺，偷来一块豆腐皮给豹子包好了腰骨。就这样，豹子得了一个“铜头铁尾豆腐腰”的绰号。

豹子为了报答乌鸦的救命之恩，无论在山冈谷地里捕得什么野兽，只要乌鸦看见，就留给它一份。

据说，从此以后，豹子再也不敢上一丈高的树捕食了，并发誓一旦抓到猫，不吃猫肉，只当板凳坐，直到把猫坐死，以报深仇大恨。

搜集整理：赵家健

编者按：用豆腐皮给豹子治疗腰骨折断，这是一个解释豹子“铜头铁尾豆腐腰”绰号的小桥段，不同的人在不同的故事中吸纳这个环节，和其他的环节构成新的故事。这样的方式，是民间故事基本的组织形态。这次是居心叵测的豹子从一开始就不怀好意地学上树的本领。老猫显然是老江湖，总是会留一手保底救命的本事。对于生活在生存边缘的人群，这些都是他们需要理解的游戏规则。人们根据衣食无忧的背景，很可能会指责故事里没有正能量，没有教孩子学好。

学好之前，先要学会生存，这才是残酷的现实。不认识这种生存式的困境，就强调一些似乎不言自明的原则，实际上把这些原则简单化、单薄化了。

The Leopard Sits on the Cat

A long time ago, leopards could only hunt on ground, and could not climb trees. One day, the leopard came sneakily to a pig's pen to drag a pig to eat. When he walked near to the fence, he saw an old cat leading a few kittens playing games under a tree. The leopard looked at them for a moment and thought that the cats had no specialty, then pounced at the old cat. The clever cat saw the leopard pounced, and screamed, "CHILDREN!" then jumped on the tree. Hearing their mom's screaming, the little kittens jumped on the tree. The leopard did not catch anyone, and got very angry. His front paw clawed and his hind legs jumped and circled around and around the tree, but he still could not climb it. The old cat sat on the tree and made no noise. As time passed, the leopard controlled himself and pleaded to the cat, "My sister cat! Sorry about today when I interrupted you. You have this special gift of moving, why not hunt animals instead playing each other?" The old cat said, "This trick we learned is not for hurting, but to help our human fellows to catch those annoying mice." The cunning leopard said, "All right! Please, sister cat, may you teach me how to climb trees so that I am also able to catch mice for the human fellows?"

When the old cat heard that the leopard wanted to help humans catch mice, she felt sad. That year when the human fellow came to fetch her from the Western Heaven, he said that the cat would only have three years to live in human's world. After she caught all the mice, she could go back to her western home. Because the old cat accidentally let one mouse slip from her mouth, now there were a lot of mice and she could not go back to the West. When recalling this, the cat promised, "Okay, I will teach you. But on one condition: when you finish learning you can only use it to catch mice. You can't hurt anyone else." For learning how to climb a tree and eating the cats, the leopard promised to do that. But the cat saw that the leopard was not sincere so the cat just taught the leopard how to climb up a tree but not how to get down a tree.

After three days of learning, the leopard wanted to eat the cats but couldn't find any excuse. He was always unhappy. The old cat had been observing the leopard's every move and was always on guard against the leopard. That day, a little kitten caught a mouse and happily brought it to the old cat. The old cat took the mouse from the kitten's mouth and handed it to the leopard. When the old cat approached the leopard, the leopard heard the cat's complaint and said to her, "Sister cat, there is a wad of cotton in your throat. I can help you take it out because it bothers you every day." With that, the leopard pounced on the old cat. The old cat said, "Ah!" and jumped up the palm tree. The leopard also jumped up to catch up with her. The leopard chased the cat to a high place. The old cat slipped down from the palm tree with a stroke of back foot and front paw, and then jumped up to a palm tree about two feet high. The leopard was eager to catch the cat, just followed the old cat. With a push on the back foot and a move on the front paw, she glided down, but the old cat didn't teach him this. As a result, he fell from the palm tree, and broke his spine. In order to give the leopard a good lesson, the old cat jumped down from the palm tree, grabbed the leopard's nose with her front paws twice until it started bleeding. The leopard heavily hurt himself and was unable to move at all. Fortunately, he was found by a black crow. The leopard begged the crow earnestly. The crow flew to a farmer's house and stole a piece of tofu to wrap the leopard's spine. In this way, the leopard got a nickname of "copper head, iron tail but tofu waist".

In order to repay the crow for saving his life, no matter what wild animals he caught in the mountains and valleys, as long as the crow saw them, he would leave them a share.

It is said that from then on, leopards would never dare to go up a tree to hunt. They vowed that once they caught the cat, they would not eat it, rather they would only sit on it as a bench until the cat died, so as to repay their deep hatred.

狮子和野猪

有一头狮子，几天没找到水喝了。有一天，它找到了一塘水，高兴极了。

与此同时，有一头野猪也在找水吃。它找了好几天才找到狮子找到的这塘水，也就喜欢得不得了。

可是，一个小小的塘子，水才那么一点点，它们都想抢先喝，争个不可开交。争着争着，两个就打起架来了。打了半天，还是一个不让一个。两个打累了就各自在树下休息。

一会儿，狮子渴得不得了，爬起来要去喝水。野猪见了就跑去咬狮子，不让它喝水。于是它们两个又厮打起来了。打累了又各自在树下睡觉。一会儿，野猪渴坏了，爬起来去喝水，狮子见了又爬起来去咬野猪。它两个又打起来了。就这样，打来打去，打打停停，停停打打，累了休息，还是互不相让，谁也吃不上水。

这时，树上有只老鹰一直在看它俩打架，希望它两个互相打死了，好吃它们的肉。就在这时，又飞来一只乌鸦在树上叫道："啊！啊！打合，打合。"

狮子抬头一看，见树上落着一只老鹰和一只乌鸦，它想了一想，对野猪说："你看看树上落着的是什么？"野猪抬头看了看，回答说："那明明是老鹰和乌鸦。"狮子又问，"你知道它两个落在树上想干什么？"野猪回答说："它两个还是想来喝老子的这塘水嘛，谁来喝都不行，这塘水是老子的，你知道吗？"狮子又对野猪说："它两个不是想喝水呀，而是想来吃我们两个的肉。要是我们两个再这样打下去，互相打死的话。它俩就来吃我们的肉了，你知道吗？"

野猪听了这话，心想：是呀，真是这样。它想着就对狮子说："我们两个别打了，再打，谁也不得喝水，还要送掉老命呢！这样吧，这水先让你喝，你喝了我再喝吧。"狮子也说："还是你先喝，我在后喝，喝完水后，我两个就走吧，别再干老鹰和乌鸦高兴的事。"狮子和野猪喝完水后就走了。老鹰生气地对乌鸦说："就是你太叫得欢了，它两个跑了。"乌鸦埋怨老鹰说:“就是你太难看了，它两个怕你的大钩子嘴才跑的。”于是乌鸦和老鹰吵起来了。

搜集：藤茂芳
整理：张亚萍

编者按：狮子与野猪，都是称霸一方的角色。在面对一个充足的水源时，为了优先喝水的权力，大打出手。这在一个经济理性人的时代，看起来不仅幼稚愚蠢，而且荒诞不经。实际上，理性人考虑的是喝到水，满足自己的身体生理需求，对于其他的部分，是考虑不周的。因为在一个传统的社会里，社会地位比物质的满足更为重要，而这种社会地位，就是通过这些优先权体现出来的。一旦放弃了某种优先权，相当于承认自己的地位低下，以后会遇到诸多难题。这也是面子在一个传统社区中具有格外重要的意义的原因。

把一只新母鸡放在一群鸡里，她需要和很多鸡打架，以此确认自己在这群鸡中的排序。一旦排序清楚，那么在摄食等行为上，就知道什么次序做什么事情。这种动物行为叫“啄序”。因为鸡群是一个垂直结构的群体。

传统社会基本上都是垂直结构的。但是现代社会是一个扁平结构，每个人按照自己的理性行动，并且预期其他人也按照这个理性行动，从而构建一个现代性的和谐。

狮子和野猪，最后意识到小人物在等着自己的灭亡，好蚕食自己的肉体，于是取得了某种妥协，并且彼此谦让。注意这个谦让一旦发生，双方都会表现出更多的谦让，实际上，这个时候谦让更多的，更可以显示出自己的身份。

而乌鸦和老鹰，代表小人物，最后开始彼此出言不逊，辱骂贬斥，这更衬托了狮子和野猪的身份超凡。

The Lion and the Boar

There was a lion who hadn't found any water to drink for a few days. One day, he finally found a pond of water and was extremely happy.

At the same time, a boar was also looking for water to drink. It took him several days to find the pool of water that the lion had found, and he was very happy too!

However, how could such a small pond, with limited water, satisfy both of them? They both wanted to drink first, fighting inseparably. After fighting for a long time, neither wanted to drink secondly. When they got tired, they rested under a tree.

For a while, the lion was thirsty for sure. He got up to drink. When the boar saw him rising up, he rushed to bite the lion and would not let him drink. So they fought again. Both tired, they rested under the tree. After a while, the boar was dying of thirst. He got up to drink water. When the lion saw this, he rose up to bite the boar. The two of them started fighting again. In this pattern, when they got tired and they took a rest. They just could not let the other go first. As a result, neither was able to drink any water.

At this time, there flew an eagle to sit on the tree and watch them fight, with a hope that they would kill each other and he could eat their meat finally. Just then, a crow came to the tree and cried, "Ah! Ah! Fight, fight!"

The lion looked up and saw the eagle and the crow on the tree. He thought about it and said to the boar, "What can you see on that tree?" The boar looked up and replied, "It's clear! An eagle and a crow." The lion asked again, "Do you know what is in their minds when they sit on the tree?" The boar replied, "Do they want to drink the water as well? You and I are still fighting over this. No one else can drink it except me! The pond belongs to me. You should have known!" The lion said to the boar, "They don't want to drink water, they want to eat you and me! If we keep fighting like this, we will kill each other and they are coming to eat us, you know that? "

When the boar heard this, he thought, "Yes, it is true." He thought about it and said to the lion, "If we keep fighting, neither can drink the water and both will die! Well, you drink the water first, and I'll drink it after you." The lion also said, "You'd better drink it first. I'll drink it later. After drinking the water, I'll go away. Don't do what the eagle and the crow are wanting us to do." The lion and the boar finished drinking and left. The eagle said angrily to the crow, "It's just because you shout too much. They are gone." The crow complained to the eagle, "It's just because you are so ugly that they are afraid of your big beak." So, the crow and the eagle started fighting.

麂子和豹子换工

相传从前动物很多，不但聪明，而且会说人话。麂子原先是一种全身雪白，十分灵便、胆子很小的动物。豹子是一种狡猾凶残，专食其他弱小兽类的动物。

有一天，麂子和豹子在路上相遇，商量换工薅地。豹子怕影响自己的生产，要麂子先帮它薅地。麂子怕豹子，就不得不答应了。每天做完活，豹子就去叼山中野兽的肉给麂子吃。豹子的地全部薅完后，豹子才去换工，帮麂子薅地。

第一天薅地，快到晌午了，豹子叫麂子拿饭来吃。麂子到水沟边找来了鲜嫩的青草，请豹子吃，豹子一见就发火了，说："你帮我薅地时，我请你吃肉；我帮你薅地，为什么不用肉来招待我呢？"麂子说："我从不杀害生灵，只用青草充饥，哪里拿肉来招待你呢？"豹子一听，圆睁双眼，露出两排獠牙，对麂子凶神恶煞地说："拿不来肉，我就先把你吃了！"麂子胆小，被豹子一吓，跳出几丈远，无奈只好再去给它找肉。

在深深的树林里，在密密的草丛中，有一个不易发现的石洞，里面豹子的两个小儿正张着嘴巴，等母豹子回来喂奶。麂子一见本不忍心杀死它们，但是，想到等着肉吃的老豹子，想到这两个小豹子长大了也同样要吃其他动物，一狠心把两个小豹子踩死了。麂子把它们的肉抬去请老豹子吃，豹子开始狼吞虎咽，没有吃出什么味道，吃完后，用舌头舔嘴巴的时候，才觉出有一股奶腥气，就问麂子："为什么这些肉里有我的奶气味？"麂子说："不知道。"豹子感到不对，就回窝里去看它的小儿，麂子趁机跑了。豹子发现窝里没有了小儿，就去追麂子。快要追上的时候，遇着一头野猪，麂子请野猪帮着评理。野猪听完豹子和麂子申辩的理由后，判定麂子无罪，它对豹子说："麂子本来是不会杀生的，这次杀死你的小儿的错误，是由于你的逼迫而造成的。"因此，野猪拦住豹子，准备把麂子放跑。豹子认为和麂子无理可讲，就龇牙咧嘴地扑向麂子。野猪看到豹子蛮横无理，也趁豹子不防，一个窝罗旋，先把豹子按翻了。麂子被吓得四腿发抖，野猪瞧见那副惊吓的样子，又好笑又可怜，便对麂子说："快来帮着些。"麂子颤巍巍地刚靠近豹子，恰好野猪咬通了豹子的脖子，红血飞溅，把雪白的麂子染得一身红色，只剩条尾巴是白色的。

搜集整理：杨叶生

编者按：强者与弱者，很可能没有真正意义上的合作，只有某种不同程度的妥协。从开始换工，就是豹子主导，而且麂子不得不听从，直到帮豹子做完豹子的地里活。现在该豹子为麂子工作，豹子挑三拣四地要吃肉，麂子又不得不设法解决。当麂子面对豹子的幼子的时候，小人物的正义感和诡诈让他做了一个残忍的决定，用幼子的肉招待母亲。野猪作为法官，为这样的两造裁决，并不容易，因为都有足够的理由。野猪最后以麂子的天性为依据判决麂子无罪，豹子不服，就想凭借自身的暴力按照自己的心意解决问题，却死在了野猪的手里。

这个故事告诫了蛮横的人，不要欺负弱小的人。也暗示了弱小者，不要与强横者合作。与自己身份相称或者近似的人合作，彼此可以牵制互利，才是合作的基础。

The Muntjac and the Leopard Exchange Their Work

It is said that there were many kinds of animals in the ancient time. They were not only smart, but also able to speak human language. Originally, a muntjac was a kind of animal with white fur, very nimble and timid. A leopard was a kind of cunning and ferocious animal that specialized in eating other weak animals.

One day, a muntjac and a leopard met on the road, and they discussed how to exchange their work to clean up the weeds in the field. The leopard was afraid that the exchange would affect yielding. So she wanted the muntjac to help weed her field first. Muntjac was afraid of leopard, so the muntjac had to agree. At the end of each working day, the leopard went to hunt wild animals for both of them to eat. After all the work in the leopard's land was finished, it came the leopard's turn to help the muntjac weed the field.

On the first day working in the muntjac's field, when it was almost noon, the leopard asked the muntjac to bring food to eat. The muntjac went to fetch some fresh green grass from the ditch for the leopard to eat. The leopard got angry at the sight of the grass and said, "When you worked in my field, I invited you to eat meat; but now when I work for you, why don't you use meat to entertain me?" the muntjac said, "I never kill living creatures. I only eat grass. How can I serve you with meat?" When the leopard heard this, she widened her eyes, showed two rows of her fangs and said to the muntjac ferociously, "If you cannot provide the meat, I will eat you first!" The muntjac was timid, frightened by the leopard leaping a few feet away, but he had no other choice but to find meat for the leopard.

In the deep woods, in the dense grass, there was an unobvious cave, in which two baby leopards were opening their mouths, waiting for the mother leopard to come back to nurse them. At first sight, the muntjac couldn't bear to kill them, but when he thought of the old leopard waiting for meat, he realized that these two little leopards would also eat other animals when they grew up. So he trampled the two little leopards to death. The muntjac carried their meat to the old leopard to eat. The leopard began to devour it, but she didn't taste anything special. After eating, when she licked her mouth, she felt that there was a smell of milk. She asked the muntjac, "Why does this meat have a smell of my milk?" The muntjac said, "I don't know." The leopard felt something wrong, and went back to her cave to see her children. The muntjac took the opportunity to escape. The leopard found that there was no child in the cave, so she went chasing the muntjac. When she was about to catch the muntjac, she ran to a boar. The muntjac asked the boar to be a judge. After hearing the story, the boar decided that the muntjac was innocent. He said to the leopard, "The muntjac would not have killed animals. The mistake of killing your children this time is caused by your persecution." Therefore, the boar stopped the leopard and prepared to let the muntjac run away. The leopard thought it was ridiculous to reason with the muntjac, so she pounced at the muntjac. When the boar saw the leopard was unreasonable, he turned the leopard over first while the leopard was not defending itself. The muntjac's legs trembled with fear. The boar saw the frightened look, feeling funny and also pitiful. He said to the muntjac, "Come and help me." The muntjac trembled and got close to the leopard. Just as the boar bit through the leopard's neck, the red blood splashed and dyed the snow-white muntjac red. Only the tail was white.

龙变穿山甲

远古时候，南山脚下有个最大最大的水塘，塘水清汪汪的，连树叶都不落一片，里面有座龙宫，老龙全都住着。南山半腰坡上住着一只兔子。有一天，天气燥热，老龙们嘴打哈欠眼睛涩，一个个耷拉着脑袋，潜在水里午睡。兔子晒烦了，就跑到龙塘边戏水。兔子泡在水里，又凉爽又安逸，高兴得“劈劈啪啪”地扑打着水嬉戏，自个儿闹腾开了。

老龙们一觉醒来，伸头往水塘边一瞄，只见一只兔子在那里玩乐，搅得水塘不得安宁。有条老龙就跑到兔子跟前教训它：“兔子！以后不准你来我们龙塘洗澡。”

兔子一听，心里老大不高兴，看看老龙张牙舞爪，蛮横不讲理的样子，十分可恨，可惜自己那么一点个儿，还不够老龙吃一嘴。它想，硬斗不过，就施软计吧。兔子灵机一动，装出一副满不在乎的神情，对老龙说：“我说老龙啊，不来就不来，没有离了和尚不吃斋，离了花大姐不上街的事。山外有山，天外有天，我去山那边洗，那儿的水塘比这个大，水比这里清，比这里好玩。老来这里耍，我也腻烦了。”

兔子一番絮叨，说动了老龙的心。老龙真以为还有更好的水塘，便说：“兔子你领我们去看看吧！”

兔子知道老龙已经上当，心里乐开了花，摆出得意的样儿，说：“要去就走，往后你们连我的影子都见不着了。”

于是，一群老龙跟着兔子上路了。走了九山十八坳，一群老龙累得气喘吁吁，问兔子水塘在什么地方，兔子总是回答：“快到了。”火辣辣的日头晒得老龙全身冒热气，老龙抬头只见光山秃岭，不见一点水影子，十分恼怒，领头的老龙张口把兔子含进嘴里，问兔子：“离水塘到底还有多远？”兔子诡计多端，说：“你张一下嘴，我看看还有多远。”老龙一张嘴，兔子赶紧蹦出来，说声：“老龙，你们等着，我去山顶望一下。”兔子去个影无踪，有去无回。

一群老龙热得忍耐不住，只好硬着头皮往土里拱，每拱一下身子都要缩短一截，七拱八拱，身子缩成了一团，头也变成又圆又小，只剩下身上的鳞甲没有变。老龙钻在土洞里，再也回不到水里了。从此，老龙变成了穿山甲，它们留在山上生活，繁衍子孙。以后，世间只剩龙塘，再也没有龙了，因为它们都变成了穿山甲。

搜集整理：赵安增

编者按：小人物兔子，又一次以狡诈和欺骗取得了胜利。相信这个骗子的老龙们，无奈之下，变成了穿山甲。孔子说，小人难养，大概就是这个意思。在追求诚信的现代社会，对于兔子这样的行为，是极其不齿的。但是在一个传统社会，小人物如果想保全自己，就需要有这样的小聪明。不了解这种文化差异，一味地指责某些人是骗子，其实是自己的无知和狭隘，没有足够的阅历和同情心，也没有读到这些民间故事。

因此，这些故事虽然未必那么三观正确，但是可以让一个人知道，不同的社会文化可能有哪些行为。知道并不等于就一定变坏，而不让知道很可能会被坏人所骗。

Dragon Becomes Pangolin

In ancient times, there was the largest pond at the foot of the Nanshan Mountain. The pond was clear and watery, even no leaves falling in it. There was a dragon palace in it, where all the old dragons lived. A rabbit lived on the hillside of the Nanshan Mountain. One day, it was hot and dry. The old dragons yawned and their eyes were astringent, with their heads hanging down one by one and taking a nap in the water. Tired of the sun, the rabbit ran to the Dragon's Pond to play water. The rabbit, soaking in the water, cool and comfortable, was so happy that he splashed and frolicked in the water, making a noise of his own.

As soon as the old dragons woke up, they stretched out their heads out of the water and saw a rabbit playing there, which made the pond ripple. An old dragon ran to the rabbit and scolded him, "Rabbit! You are not allowed to take a bath in the Dragon's Pond."

When the rabbit heard this, he was not happy. He looked at the old dragon's arrogant and unreasonable appearance, which was very hateful. Unfortunately, he was a little bit too small for the old dragon to eat. He thought that although he could not fight directly against them, he could use indirect tactics. The rabbit had an idea, pretending, to be indifferent, and he said to the old dragon, "Hi, old dragon! If you don't want me to come, I won't come. There is no way for a person to starve without the help of the monk, or stop going to the market without beautiful clothes. If you don't leave the monk, you won't eat. If you leave the big sister, you won't go to the street. There is a mountain beyond the mountain. There is a sky beyond this sky. I will go to the the other mountain, I'll go wash there. The water is cleaner than here. It's more fun than here. I'm tired of playing here all the time anyway."

What the rabbit said moved the old dragon. The dragon thought there was a better pond, so he said, "Rabbit, please show it to us!"

The rabbit knew that the old dragon had been cheated. He was happy inside and put on a proud look. He said, “If you want to go, go with me right away. After all, you will never see my shadow again in the future.”

So, a group of old dragons followed the rabbit on the road. After nine mountains and eighteen hollows, the group of old dragons were very tired and panting. When they asked rabbit where the pond was, the rabbit always replied, “We are almost there.” The hot sun made old dragons’ whole-body steam. They looked up and only saw the bare mountains but no water shadow. They were very angry. The leader of dragons held the rabbit in his mouth and asked the rabbit, “How far is it apart from the pond?” The rabbit was crafty and said, “Open your mouth and let me see how far it is.” As soon as the old dragon opened his mouth, the rabbit jumped out and said, “Wait here, old dragon. I’ll go to the top of the mountain and have a look.” The rabbit was gone without a trace.

The group of old dragons couldn’t bear the heat, so they had to bend their heads into the earth. Every time they arched, their bodies were shortened. The more arches they did, the shorter their bodies became. Until finally their bodies shrunk into a mass, and their heads had become round and small. Only the scales on their bodies remained unchanged. The old dragons drilled holes in the earth, but could never go back to the water. Since then, dragons became pangolins, living in the mountain and multiplying there. After that, there was only dragon ponds in the world, no dragons any more, because they all became pangolins.

立春后穿山甲钻洞格外深

从前有一对新婚夫妇，男的名叫李贵荣。他们有片稻田，坐落在山坳旁边。立春刚过，李贵荣就扛起犁，吆着牛去田里做活。

中午突然下起雨来，俗话说：头发雨，淋不得。李贵荣又没戴蓑衣帽子，只得把犁扎好，跑到田边的一个洞里躲雨。说来也奇怪，洞里放着一张穿山甲的皮，李贵荣看斜雨淋进洞里，真有点春寒料峭，不禁打了个冷战，就顺手理起穿山甲皮披在身上。

雨过天晴，李贵荣准备去犁田。人不错为仙，马不错为龙。他伸手去揭穿山甲皮，哪料到，穿山甲皮已紧紧贴在身上，他使出了吃奶的力气，也没有揭下来。恰巧李贵荣的妻子，提着篮子送晌午饭来了。妻子看见插在田中间的犁，知道丈夫没去多远，就“李贵荣，李贵荣”地喊起来。他听到妻子的叫声，急得手忙脚乱，他怕自己的丑模样吓坏妻子，也怕别人看见闹一辈子笑话，就往洞里钻，也怪，李贵荣披着穿山甲皮，轻而易举地就钻到土里去了。外面妻子一声接一声叫，他往土里越钻越深。

李贵荣的妻子，从晌午叫到天黑，不见丈夫的面，伤心气绝，就死在田边。传说，她变成一只雀，每当立春后，就飞到山间田边，去寻找自己心爱的丈夫。它蹲在树梢上，一边东张西望，一边凄惨悲切地叫着：“李贵荣，李贵荣！”

据说立春后，这种雀一叫，穿山甲就钻得特别深，一般都很难挖到它。

讲述：杨从根

搜集整理：孙加申

编者按：这个故事异常精彩，几乎不逊于卡夫卡的《变形记》。在卡夫卡的作品里，主人公一觉醒来，变成一只甲虫，之后一家人的关系因为这次变形而开始变形，最终以主人公死去，全家恢复了往日的宁静结局。日常生活的宁静，其实是一种残忍。

还有两部作品也被称为《变形记》。古罗马诗人奥维德的《变形记》，以 250 个故事描述了罗马和希腊神话世界之中的历史，成为后世取之不尽的艺术泉源。

而古罗马作家阿普列尤斯创作的《变形记》又名《金驴记》，有 11 卷之多，写一个沉迷魔法的年轻人吃了一种药物变成驴子，经历千辛万苦，最终恢复人形。这是唯一完整地流传至今的古罗马小说，对于后世的作品影响很大。

阿昌族的穿山甲与山雀故事，虽然简单，但是动人心弦，把每个人物的心理和行为刻画得栩栩如生。这样，一个恋慕丈夫的妻子，一个羞涩内向的丈夫，在一次意外之后，发生了一连串的变故，最后成为生生世世的悲情。

Pangolins Dig Deeper In the Beginning of Spring

Long ago, there was a newly-married couple. The husband's name was Guirong Li. They had a piece of land in a valley. The Beginning of Spring had just passed and Guirong Li went to plow the field with his cow and rake.

One afternoon, it suddenly began to rain. There was a saying goes: One should not get his hair wet. Guirong Li didn't have a hat so he had to put away the rake and ran to a cave nearby to hide. It was so weird that there was a pangolin skin in the cave. Guirong Li watched the rain creeping into the cave. It felt really cold and he started to shiver, then he put on the pangolin skin.

When the rain was over, Guirong Li was getting ready to go back to work. If humans didn't make mistakes, then they were immortals. If horses didn't make mistakes, then they were Chinese dragons. He raised his hand to pull off the pangolin skin, but he was not able to pull it off. He used all his strength but it did not work. Right at that time, his wife came over to give him his lunch. His wife saw the rake there and that means he was still nearby, so she started shouting his name "Guirong Li, Guirong Li!". He heard his wife's voice and became rigid. He was afraid that his ugly look would scare his wife, and also others might make fun of him. So he drilled into the cave. Weirdly, it was really easy to drill with the pangolin skin. His wife called out to him. But the more she yelled, the deeper he drilled into the cave.

Guirong Li's wife called out to him from noon to night but still did not hear any answer. She was really sad and died on the edge of the field. Legend says that she has turned into a sparrow. In the Begining of Spring, she would go to the field and call out to her beloved husband. She will sit on a branch, look everywhere and call out "Guirong Li, Guirong Li."

Legends has it that when this kind of sparrow comes, mandolins drill deeper. It usually won't be found.

穿山甲把身子蜷成一团的来由

古老的时候，禽兽都会讲话，而且会自己修房盖屋，蒸饭酿酒，都像人类一样生活着。那时候，乌鸦专营酿酒生意。别看它全身漆黑一团，可酿出的酒醇香可口，禽兽们都争相购买。穿山甲可是一个大名鼎鼎的醉鬼，每街必饮，每饮必醉，而且蛮横不讲理，有钱它要喝三碗，无钱也要饮三盅。没有钱，就说先赊着。乌鸦虽然给它记着账，可穿山甲也圆滑，它知道账虽记着，可无人作证，便想赖账，说它没有喝过乌鸦的酒，是乌鸦诓骗它，硬给它记上去的，概不承认。乌鸦遇上这么一个倒霉鬼，感到十分伤脑筋。

有一次，乌鸦背着酒罐到集市出售，路上正好遇着它的好朋友画眉雀，它们一路同行。到了市场，乌鸦刚摆好酒摊，皮厚老脸的穿山甲向着酒摊蹒跚走来。乌鸦汲取了以往的教训，就对画眉雀说："朋友，我打酒给穿山甲喝，你帮记着一个斤两，作个证明吧。"画眉雀点头表示应承。乌鸦给穿山甲斟一次酒，就高声念一下盅数，画眉雀就在一旁记录着。

穿山甲喝了一盅又一盅，糖是越吃越腻，酒是越喝越甜，一直喝了二十二盅半，已经酩酊大醉，头晕眼花，穿山甲提起脚步就要走。这回乌鸦可要跟它算账了。乌鸦说：

"喂！你的酒钱还没有给呢！"

穿山甲自己也记不清喝了多少酒，便问：

"我喝了多少酒？"

画眉雀连忙回答："九十两。"

穿山甲想赖账，说："我没有喝这么多酒呀！"

"九十两，九十两……。"画眉雀生气了，连三接四地叫起来。禽兽们听到叫声，都莫名其妙，一个个围拢来看热闹。穿山甲酒醉心明白，眼看大伙都围着看，要是乌鸦把平时自己赖账的丑事，兜底儿掀出来，那就会把脸都丢尽。穿山甲赶忙想了一个脱身之计：它把头弯下，用身子和尾巴把头包起来蜷缩成一团滚在地上。

乌鸦看了穿山甲的那副丑相心下生气，就跑过去，用尖嘴往穿山甲身上接二连三地啄，用脚往穿山甲身上一阵猛踢。可是碰到的尽是些硬壳壳，实在没有办法。乌鸦只好无可奈何地“啊，啊！”地叫了几声，叹着气作罢。

如今，只要画眉雀看见穿山甲，就情不自禁地“九十两，九十两！”地喊起来，而穿山甲一听到画眉雀叫，也认为画眉雀出来证明它喝了乌鸦九十两酒，乌鸦会来讨酒钱，急得把身躯缩成一团。

讲述：孙加金

搜集整理：孙加申

编者按：动物众生相，无外乎人间。人中有酒色之徒，沉迷杯中物，不可自拔。这样的人，既可气，又可笑。可气在于一旦酒瘾上来，就一发不可收拾，直至烂醉如泥。之后又借酒发疯，肆无忌惮。虽然知道这样不好，却总是不能改过自新。可笑在于酒后的言行幼稚粗鲁，暴露出隐藏的一面来。

穿山甲好酒，偏偏又赖账，这样的人，你我身边总是有那么几个。饮酒后付钱，这是一个集市上的规矩，乌鸦不能为了穿山甲之前的行为，改变这个规矩。但是穿山甲酒后赖账，让乌鸦采用了人证的手段。这里是画眉鸟做了这个证人。这次穿山甲被揭穿之后，不能否认自己饮酒，那就做缩头乌龟吧，把自己蜷起来，不闻不问，不管不顾。

可能我们身边的那几个酒鬼，也知道穿山甲这样的故事，当他们每次饮酒之前，都会有人用这个故事逗他。如同人们逗弄孔乙己一样，“孔乙己，你又偷了东西。”

The Reason for the Pangolin Curling up

In ancient times, beasts and animals can speak, and they can build their own houses, steam rice and make wine, and all live like humans. At that time, the crow specialized in brewing business. Regardless of the dark mass appearance, the brewed wine was so delicious that the beasts were competing to buy it. The pangolin was famous drunkard who must drink on every street and every drink must be drunk, so he was very unreasonable. If he had money, he would drink three bowls, and if he had little money, he would drink three cups. If he had no money, he paid credit instead. Although the crow kept an account for him, the pangolin was cunning enough to deny the account, saying that he had not drunk the crow's wine for there was no proof at all. The crow encountered such an unlucky ghost and felt very nervous.

On one occasion, the crow carried wine bottles to the market for sale. On the way, he happened to meet his good friend the thrush, and they walked along the way. At the market, the crow had just set up the wine stall, and the thick-skinned pangolin staggered towards the wine stall. The crow learned the lessons from the past, so he said to the thrush, "Friend, I'll let the pangolin drink it. You help me remember it and make a written account as proof." The thrush nodded and promised. The crow poured the pangolin and counted the cup loudly for each pour, and the thrush recorded it.

The pangolin drank one cup after another. The sugar became more and more greasy, and the wine drank more and more sweet. He had been drinking for twenty-two and a half cups. He was drunk and dizzy. This time the crow was going to settle accounts with him. The crow said:

"Hey! Haven't you paid your money!"

The pangolin could not remember how much wine he had drunk, so he asked:

"How much wine did I drink?"

The thrush quickly replied, “Ninety Liang.”

The pangolin wanted to pay the bill and said, “I didn’t drink that much!”

“Ninety Liang, ninety Liang ...” The thrush was angry and cried out in succession. The beasts were all baffled when they heard the crying, and they looked around one by one to see the excitement. The pangolin was drunk but he knew in mind that everyone was looking at them and if the crow mentioned the scandals of his usual delinquency, he would lose his face. The pangolin immediately thought of an escape plan: he bent his head down, wrapped his head with his body and tail, curled up in a ball and rolled himself on the ground.

The crow looked angrily at the pangolin and ran over to him pecking the pangolin with his pointed mouth and kicking him with his feet. But all he encountered was hard shells and there was really no soft place on the pangolin’s curled body. The crow had no choice but to cry “Ah, ah!” And sighed.

Now, as long as the thrush sees the pangolin, he can’t help shouting, “Ninety Liang, ninety Liang!” And the pangolin hears the thrush, thinking that the thrush is out to prove the crow’s ninety Liang of wine and the crow will come to ask for money, then he will anxiously shrink his body.

知了为什么没嘴巴和肠子

传说过去知了的肠子又粗又长，每天要吃很多东西；知了的嘴巴也很长，它叫起来，几山几坳都听得见。有一天早上，麂子在自己的窝里呼呼熟睡，一个知了飞到麂子窝边张嘴大叫，叫声吓醒了麂子，一骨碌跳起来，拼命乱跑，踩着了老鼠的洞。老鼠以为有人挖它的洞，急忙从后洞逃进了阿昌人种的瓜地里，老鼠不小心咬断了瓜藤，瓜藤上的老瓜带着瓜藤滚下了山脚。老瓜滚进阿昌人种的芝麻地里，摇落了芝麻籽，芝麻籽恰好掉进了利柴鸡的眼睛里。利柴鸡睁不开眼睛，什么也看不见，"扑拉拉"扇动翅膀乱飞，利柴鸡歇在一棵枯树桩上揉眼睛，跳翻了枯树桩，树桩正好打在葫芦蜂的蜂包上。葫芦蜂以为有人烧它的蜂包，就乱飞乱叮，一下子叮着了大象的长鼻子。大象发急了，它用鼻子扯倒大树，抬起石桩般的四条粗腿乱踩。正好大兵过路，有的被打伤，有的被踩死了。士兵们把老象包围起来，问它为什么把兵将踩死了？老象说："要问就得去问葫芦蜂，是它叮了我的鼻子，我才乱踩"。士兵带着老象去找葫芦蜂，葫芦蜂说："因为利柴鸡踩翻枯树桩砸了我的蜂包，我才错叮了大象的鼻子，这是利柴鸡的责任"。他们找到利柴鸡，问它为什么要踩翻树桩去砸蜂包？利柴鸡说："应该由老鼠负责，是它咬断瓜藤，老瓜摇落芝麻籽，芝麻籽掉进我的眼睛里，我看不见乱飞，才踩翻了树桩。"他们找到老鼠，问老鼠为什么要咬断瓜藤？老鼠说："这不能怪我，要问就问麂子，是它踩烂了我的洞，我跑到瓜地里，才咬断了瓜藤。"麂子跑来解释说："是知了乱叫，把我从梦中吓醒，才踩了老鼠的洞，这个罪应该由知了负责。"他们一起去找知了，知了结结巴巴地想要赖账。大家很气愤，集体商定：用抽去知了的肚肠，封住知了的嘴巴的办法来处罚它，使它以后不得吃东西，不能大声乱叫。从此以后，知了没有了肚肠，没有了嘴巴。这时候，它才明白了自己的错误，扇动翅膀，痛苦地呻吟："知了""知了"。

搜集整理：杨叶生

编者按：这就是阿昌族版的蝴蝶效应。一只知了的一次鸣叫，引发了一系列的后果，好像多米诺骨牌一样，最终导致了人命案。人命案需要追责，之后就是逻辑链条上的上溯，所有的行为都有其原因，而到了知了这里，已经找不到借口了。于是就惩罚知了，让它学会不要乱喊乱叫。

的确，一句不当的言语，经过几次转述，很可能失真，并且完全变形到产生巨大而恶劣后果的水平上。如果能够约束自己的言辞，谨守口舌，就可以避免不少这样的坏事发生。

Why Cicada Has No Mouth or Intestines

According to the legend, the cicada's intestines were thick and long and he ate a lot of food every day. Besides, the cicada's mouth was also very long. If he cried, he could be heard in several mountains and concaves. One morning, a muntjac was sleeping soundly in his cozy cave. A cicada flew to the side of the muntjac's cave and opened his mouth to sing. The sound awakened the muntjac. He jumped up and ran out stepping on a mouse's hole. The mouse thought that someone had dug his hole and hurriedly escaped from the back hole into the melon field of the Achang people. The mouse accidentally bit off the melon vine and a mature melon fell off the vine and rolled down to the foot of the mountain. The melon rolled into a sesame field of the Achang people and shook the sesame seeds off, which just fell into the eyes of a pheasant. The pheasant couldn't open his eyes and could not see anything. "Pulala" he incited his wings to fly and finally rested on a dead tree stump rubbing his eyes. He jumped over the dead tree stump, and which just hit a gourd beehive. The bees thought that someone had burned their beehive so they flew around and stung an elephant's long trunk. The elephant was anxious. He snatched down a big tree with his trunk and lifted up four thick legs like stone piles. Just at that time, many soldiers were crossing the road. Some were injured and some were trampled to death. The soldiers surrounded the old elephant and asked why he had trampled the soldiers to death. The old elephant said, "If you want to know the reason, you have to ask the gourd bees, because they stung my trunk, I started stepping around blindly." The soldiers took the old elephant to find the gourd bees. The gourd bees said, "Because a pheasant stepped on the stump and smashed our beehive, we finally stung the elephant's trunk. This is the pheasant's responsibility." They found the pheasant and asked why he stepped on the stump to smash the beehive. The pheasant said, "The mouse should be responsible, because he bit off the melon and vine, the melon shook down the sesame seeds, and the sesame seeds fell into my eyes. I can't see, flying, so overturned the stump." They found the mouse and ask why the mouse bit off the melon and vine? The mouse said, "You should not blame me. If you want to ask, ask the muntjac. He stomped my hole. I ran into the melon field and bit off the vine." The muntjac rushed over and explained, "I know. A screaming frightened me from my dreams, and then I stepped on the mouse hole. The cicada should be responsible for this case." They went to find the cicada.The cicada stuttered and did not want to pay the bill. Everyone was very angry, and collectively agreed: as a punishment the intestines of the cicada need to be removed and his mouth will be sealed to prevent him from eating and yelling loudly in the future. Since then, the cicada has neither intestines nor mouth. Only then did he understand his mistake inciting his wings, and moaning painfully "Zhiliao", "Zhiliao" (which means "Understood" in Chinese, so his Chinese nick name is "Understood".

古时选鸟王的故事

在古老的时候，猫头鹰和乌鸦两个都想着要当鸟王，它两个就出面召集各种各样的鸟在大山上的林子里开会，商量要选举一个鸟当王的事。

它们就对大伙说：“朋友们，你们都知道各种各样的蜜蜂都有一个王，所以它们很是齐心协力地做事。我们这个鸟类还没有王，做事就不如蜜蜂了。我们应该有个王，大家来商量一下，选举一个鸟王。大家的意见怎么样。”通过商量，大家七选八选地选了一下，没有结果。

有的提出来要猫头鹰来当鸟王，乌鸦听了以后，心里很不安。因为它想当鸟王，它就不同意猫头鹰来当鸟王。它说：“猫头鹰当鸟王可害怕呀，它的鼻子又勾，眼睛又大，像老猫一样，我不同意。”乌鸦第一个提出不同意。

有的就提出来叫乌鸦当鸟王，乌鸦这时心里很高兴，心想着怕得当鸟王了。猫头鹰这时提出不同意乌鸦当鸟王的意见。猫头鹰说：“乌鸦它的身子黑，连心也黑，这种鸟当鸟王，大家都活不成。”猫头鹰刚说完，乌鸦就跟它吵了起来。

它两个吵得不可开交的时候，猫头鹰不耐烦跟它吵了，就飞走了。乌鸦也就跟着飞起一直追着吵呀，追呀、追，追到另一个山林里，猫头鹰就躲起来。白天不敢出来，怕被乌鸦看见又跟它吵，报它的仇。从那以后，猫头鹰白天就一直在森林里躲着不敢出来，到夜晚才敢出来。

事情过了很久，可是有一次，乌鸦好久没有水喝了，到了口太渴的时候，到哪里找水都没有水。

乌鸦飞到一户人家，人家都把门关得紧紧的，它就从房子的屋山墙洞里飞进去找水，可是还是找不到水缸，碰到一个油罐，它以为是水了，就钻进油罐里面去，因为油太滑了，它一踩滑，就落到油罐里去了。它七挣八挣，才挣了出来，可是飞不得了。只好又找到猫头鹰说好话，请猫头鹰帮忙想个办法。它说：“猫头鹰大哥，以前的事真对不起你了，请你不要见怪吧，现在请你帮帮忙，我口渴得厉害，去找水喝，水是找不到，误入了人家的油罐，身上染得一身是油，现在飞不得了，你帮想个办法，要怎么办好。”

猫头鹰一见乌鸦就生气，还记着它的仇，因为乌鸦纠缠它好长时间，

使它白天不敢出来跟其他的鸟活动，只能在夜里独个儿活动，因此，猫头鹰就借此机会整它一下，于是给乌鸦出了个坏点子，猫头鹰说：“你身上的这个油嘛，用水也洗不掉，不知道怎么办了，只有一个办法：去烤火，烤火才能把油烘化，你的翅膀才能干，你才能飞得起来。”

乌鸦听了猫头鹰的话后，就在火塘边烤火，烤呀，转过来烤，转过去烤，烤着烤着，心太急了，想要一下子就将油烤化掉。于是就挨近火烤，一挨近火，它的翅膀上有油，就着火烧起来，周身都燃了火。乌鸦本来就黑了，加上被火这么一烧，以后就更加黑了。

乌鸦知道上了猫头鹰的当，由此，乌鸦到现在一直都在恨着猫头鹰，跟猫头鹰结下了大仇，一直见不得猫头鹰，偶尔一见到猫头鹰，就有很多乌鸦飞来围攻它，追赶它，啄它。

讲述：石老四
翻译：藤茂芳
整理：张亚萍

编者按：乌鸦是一种很聪明的鸟，也很好斗。虽然乌鸦不像猫头鹰那样是一种猛禽，但是乌鸦经常与各种猛禽搏斗，还善于围攻，以多欺少。

在阿昌族生活的区域，社会的组织程度不高，依靠世袭的权力没有多少，更多是以家庭为单位，或者家族为团体，进行生产和生活。但是在这样松散的社会中，仍然有人希望称王称霸，建立世俗性的权力。那么，这样有野心的人，就会想办法纠集大家，希望认可他的权力。对于王权的竞争，他们没有什么施政的纲领，于是，竞争集中到人品上，甚至外貌也是重要的。在这样的比较中，彼此恶语相向，造成两败俱伤。

而乌鸦和猫头鹰的争霸，导致两种鸟儿水火不容。实际上自由自在的鸟儿本来就不会接受一个鸟王的存在。但是他们都认为对方才是自己落选的原因，不仅没有达成目的，反而多了一个仇家。而开始猫头鹰躲开乌鸦，变成夜行性的鸟，看似输了一局。但是很快就借着乌鸦的一次落难，猫头鹰设计陷害了乌鸦。

这样钩心斗角的人际关系，是到处都有的，可这个故事说得直接而不露骨，殊为不易。

The Story of Choosing the King of Birds in Ancient Times

In ancient times, the owl and the crow both thought of being the king of birds. The two of them came forward to summon a variety of birds to meet in the forest on the mountain, and discussed the election of a bird to be the king.

They said to everyone, "Friends, you all know that all kinds of bees have a king, so they are working cooperatively. Our birds have no king and this makes our work not as good as the bees. We should have a king. Everyone, let's discuss and elect a bird king. How about your opinion?" Through consultation, they selected this and that, while coming to no result.

Some proposed to ask the owl to be the king of birds. After hearing this, the crow became very uneasy. Because he wanted to be the king of the birds, he disagreed with the owl as the bird king. He said, "It's scary to let an owl to be the bird king. His nose is hooked and his eyes are big. Like an old cat, I disagree." The crow first disagreed.

Some proposed to call the crow the king of the birds, and the crow was very happy at the moment, thinking that he might become the king of the birds. The owl then disagreed with this opinion. The owl said, "The crow is black and even his heart is black. If this kind of bird became the king of birds, no one can live." As soon as the owl finished, the crow quarreled with him.

When the two of them were too quarrelsome, the owl got tired and flew away. The crow followed him and flew, chasing and arguing, chasing, chasing, and chasing into another mountain forest, and the owl hid. The owl dared not come out during the day, afraid of being seen by the crow, arguing with him, and the crow taking revenge. Since then, the owl had been hiding in the forest during the day and dared not come out, only by night did he dare come out.

Things had been like this for a long time, until one day, the crow did not have any water. He was so thirsty that he had to go out to find water.

The crow flew to a family, but they closed the door tightly. So he flew in from the gable hole of the house to find water, but still couldn't find any water tank, but came across an oil tank. He thought it was water so he drilled into the oil tank.The oil is so slippery that he slipped and fell into the oil tank. He tried and tried, finally he came out of the tank but couldn't fly. He had to find the owl again to say sweet words to him in order to get some idea from the owl. He said, "Brother owl, I'm so sorry for what has happened in the past. Please don't be upset any more. Now, please help me. I'm so thirsty. I went to find water to drink. The water was not found but I slipped into people's oil tank. My wings are stained with oil, and now I can't fly. Can you find a way to solve this problem?"

The owl was angry at the sight of the crow, and remembered his bitterness, because the crow has been entangled with him for such a long time that he did not dare to come out with other birds during the day and can only act alone at night. Therefore, the owl took this opportunity to take revenge. He made a bad idea for the crow, saying, "The oil on your body can't be washed away with water. It won't help at all. There is only one way: go to the fire and the fire will melt the oil, then your wings can get dry and you can fly."

After listening to the owl's suggestion, the crow flew over to a fire pit. He turned here and there wishing the oil could be melt at once. So he walked closer to the fire, and when he got close to the fire, having oil on his wings, his body immediately burned on fire. The crow was originally black, and when he was burnt by fire, he became even darker ever since.

The crow realized that the owl had cheated him. Therefore, the crow has always hated the owl and formed a great hatred with the owl. He does not want to meet the owl. Occasionally, when crows see a owl, they come to siege him chasing and pecking him.

拖白练[1]借锦衣

从前，山鸽子有一件花纹鲜艳的锦缎衣裳，而拖白练穿的是色泽单调的灰色麻布衣。有一天，拖白练找山鸽子交朋友。它们无话不说，相处得十分融洽。山鸽子对拖白练是真心相待，推心置腹。可是拖白练则不然，它羡慕山鸽子那件色彩斑斓的锦衣，它更是嫉妒山鸽子的漂亮；它处心积虑地想把山鸽子的美丽锦衣弄到手，而在没有得到之前，又装出若无其事的样子。

有一天，拖白练终于有了法子。它飞到山鸽子旁边，佯装忧心忡忡的面孔，对山鸽子说："好朋友啊，好朋友！你是我的心肝朋友。我明天要去姑妈家吃酒席。你看，我身上穿的是灰麻布衣，多寒酸，客人会笑话我的。咳，鸽子姐姐，把你的锦衣借给我穿一次吧。"山鸽子心慈耳软，信以为实，说声"你吃完酒筵就还来"。山鸽子把自己身上的锦衣脱下来，交给了拖白练，又从拖白练手里接过灰麻布衣，穿在自己身上。拖白练穿上锦衣，梳梳翎毛，抖抖身子，拖着长尾巴，飘飘然地飞往远处树林子里去了。

过了很久，山鸽子不见拖白练来还锦衣，就飞着去寻找拖白练要锦衣。有一天，终于找到了。拖白练没等山鸽子张口，就忙不迭声地说："鸽子姐姐，你我是好朋友。真对不起！你的锦衣已经粘在我身上了，咋个也脱不下来了。你心宽点，我们就换穿了吧。"山鸽子这才恍然明白，自己上了拖白练的当。山鸽子十分气恼，当场就痛骂了拖白练一顿。可是，拖白练一点也不觉得羞耻，反倒显得沾沾自喜，张大嘴巴，"金灿灿、金灿灿……"地狂叫起来。山鸽子穿着一件灰色的麻布衣，既伤心又悔恨，经常蹲在树枝上，"裹尸裹骨，裹尸裹骨"地嘟囔着，责骂拖白练不讲信义，骗走了它的锦衣。

今天，山鸽子依然身着铅灰色的麻布衣，而拖白练却披着一件花锦

---

[1] 拖白练是当地的俗称，中文名是亚洲绶带鸟，也称亚洲天堂鸟，寿带鸟，长尾鹟，一枝花等；英文名是 Asian paradise flycather; 学名是 Terpsiphone paradisi。

衣，不管飞到哪里，都听到它扬扬自得的喊叫声。

讲述：赵启广
搜集整理：杨叶生　孙加申

编者按：可能无论是孩子或者大人，看到这个故事，都会认为拖白练死不要脸，而且蛮不讲理。如果问发生了这种事情怎么办，很多人会诉之以法，希望用法律的手段解决问题。现代人对于法律有一种信仰，而这其实不是传统社会的习惯。现代人习以为常的各种权利意识，都不是天然的，而是文化的塑造。因此，不能用大家习惯的思维去理解和应对这样的故事。

山鸽子很天真地和心怀叵测的拖白练交友。最终的结果是丢失了引以为傲的彩衣，而拖白练却喜洋洋地展示自己的战利品。对于拖白练来说，偷来的、抢来的、骗来的，其实都一样，和我们认为买来的一样理直气壮。

因为在很多传统里，偷摸拐骗都是本事，甚至比买的还要荣誉。你可以不接受这样的价值观，但是你不能否认有这样的价值观，也应该反思一下自己认为理所当然的价值观是不是真的那么合理。可能从自然界看来，人类对于生态环境的剥削利用比这些偷摸拐骗更无耻和邪恶。

Flycatcher Borrows Beautiful Clothes

In the past, the mountain pigeons had brightly patterned brocade clothes, while the flycatchers dressed in gray linen clothes with a monotone color. One day, one flycatcher found a mountain pigeon to make friends. They got along very well without many words between them. The mountain pigeon was sincere to the flycatcher. But it was not the case with the flycatcher. He envied the colorful brocade of the mountain pigeon, and he was even more jealous of the beauty of the mountain pigeon. He was deliberately trying to get the beautiful brocade of mountain pigeons, and pretended to be casual before it was available.

One day, the flycatcher finally got a way. He flew to the mountain pigeon, pretending to have a worried face, and said to the mountain pigeon, "Good friend, good friend! You are my sweetheart friend. I'm going to the aunt's house tomorrow for dinner. Look, my gray linen cloth is so shabby, and the guests will laugh at me. Come, sister pigeon, lend me your brocade to wear it once." The mountain pigeon was kind and soft-hearted, believing him and said, "You will pay me back after you eat the feast. Come." The mountain pigeon took off her brocade and handed it over to the flycatcher. Then he took the gray linen cloth from his hand and put it on herself. The flycatcher put on the colorful beautiful clothes, combed his quills, shook his body, dragged his long tail, and flew into the woods in the distance.

After a long time, the mountain pigeon still didn't see the flycatcher return her brocade, so she flew to find the flycatcher. One day, she finally found him. Without waiting for the mountain pigeon to open her mouth, he said in a hurry: "Sister pigeon, you and I are good friends. I'm so sorry! Your brocade has already stuck to me and I can't take it off. Your heart is broad. Let's exchange it." The mountain pigeon suddenly realized that she had been cheated by him. The mountain pigeon was very annoyed. However, the flycatcher did not feel shameful at all; instead, he seemed complacent and opened his mouth wide, yelling "Glory, glory..." The mountain pigeon wearing gray linen clothes was sad and regretful. She often squatted on the branch, muttering "Wrapped with bones, wrapped with bones", scolded for the flycatcher's being indifferent and unfaithful and deceived her brocade.

Today, the mountain pigeon is still dressed in lead-gray linen clothes, but the flycatcher is dressed in a flower brocade. No matter where he flies, you can hear his complacent shouting.

谷工鸟与塔拉雀

在阿昌族生活地区，流传着这样一句话：谷工鸟下蛋，塔拉雀抱蛋一场空。原来，谷工鸟和塔拉雀是很好的朋友。谷工鸟生性懒惰，老盖不好房子。塔拉雀就常常邀约谷工鸟到自己家玩。

春天到了，百鸟都忙着繁殖后代。塔拉雀也下了蛋，在家忙着抱蛋。只有谷工鸟，还是这里飞飞，那里逛逛，嘻嘻哈哈地叫着："哥哥，哥哥……"

一天，谷工鸟到塔拉雀家里玩。塔拉雀对谷工鸟说："谷工姐姐，你也应该盖间房子了，不要整天在外面逛了。不然，等小侄儿侄女们出世时，没有房子住咋个整呀？"

谷工鸟听了塔拉雀的话只微微一笑，不当回事。过了一会儿，谷工鸟又飞到林子里喊："哥哥，哥哥……"塔拉雀听了，无可奈何地摇摇头。

太阳出山两竹竿高时，塔拉雀有事出门去了。谷工鸟见了，就悄悄地溜进塔拉雀家里，把塔拉雀的蛋吃了几个，就把自己的蛋下在塔拉雀的窝里，然后又悄悄地溜走了。

因为谷工鸟的蛋和塔拉雀的蛋都是翠绿色的，所以塔拉雀没有发觉谷工鸟在自己窝里下了蛋。塔拉雀把蛋抱啊，抱啊……白天抱，夜里也抱。好不容易把红红的小宝宝抱出世了。小塔拉雀出世后，它又忙着到处找食物给小宝宝吃。

一天、两天过去了，十天、半月过去了，小宝宝身上长出了细毛。一个月过去了，小宝宝身上的毛长齐了，跟着妈妈学飞了。

谷工鸟看着自己的孩子长大了，很想去领回来，可是又不好意思对塔拉雀说。它眉头一皱，想出了一个鬼主意：对！到鸟王那里去告状。鸟王听了谷工鸟的控告，派兵把塔拉雀传进宫里。鸟王问："塔拉雀，你咋个这样霸道，把谷工鸟的娃娃也抢了！"

塔拉雀听了莫名其妙。它向鸟王申辩道："大王，我没有抢过谷工鸟的娃娃，那明明是我自己的宝宝呀！"

"把原告传来！"鸟王命令道。

几个卫兵把谷工鸟带到鸟王面前。"谷工鸟，你咋个乱说塔拉雀抢了你的娃娃？"鸟王问道。

谷工鸟翻脸不认朋友，拉下脸说："大王，塔拉雀真的抢了我的娃娃呀。"

塔拉雀看了谷工鸟一眼，气愤地说："请你摸摸良心再说话，哪个抢过你的娃娃？你可别乱陷害好人呀！"

"大王，我说的句句是实话。塔拉雀把我的娃娃抢走了，我求你给我做主。"谷工鸟跪在鸟王面前，装出十分伤心的样子说。

鸟王断不下案，就派兵到塔拉雀家里，把塔拉雀窝里的娃娃全部带进宫里，排起队站在大厅上，叫谷工鸟和塔拉雀站在他们的前面。

"现在我来断案。大家看好，这些小雀，像谷工鸟的就是谷工鸟的娃娃，像塔拉雀的就是塔拉雀的娃娃。这下你们该没有什么吵的了。"鸟王大声宣布说。

结果：四个小雀中，像谷工鸟的有三个，像塔拉雀的只有一个。谷工鸟得意地领着三个小谷工鸟走了。这下塔拉雀才明白过来。它狠狠地骂道："无耻！"

从此，塔拉雀和谷工鸟结下了冤仇。塔拉雀一见谷工鸟，就喊伙伴们："这有，这有……"伙伴们一听见喊声就连忙从窝里飞出来去追赶谷工鸟。

讲述：赵启祥
搜集整理：赵洪顺

编者按：谷工鸟就是布谷鸟，学名是大杜鹃。杜鹃名字很多，子规、杜宇都是经常用的名字，有人统计有 37 种名字。杜鹃在鸟类里鹃形目中杜鹃科的鸟，叫孵卵寄生动物，就是把自己的卵产在其他种类的鸟巢里，让其他鸟帮助孵化和喂养。这种动物行为很早就被人类观察到了，诗人杜甫写过著名的《杜鹃行》，抄录如下：

君不见昔日蜀天子，化作杜鹃似老乌。
寄巢生子不自啄，群鸟至今与哺雏。
虽同君臣有旧礼，骨肉满眼身羁孤。
业工窜伏深树里，四月五月偏号呼。
其声哀痛口流血，所诉何事常区区。
尔岂摧残始发愤，羞带羽翮伤形愚。
苍天变化谁料得，万事反复何所无。
万事反复何所无，岂忆当殿群臣趋。

杜甫写“寄巢生子不自啄，群鸟至今与哺雏”，就是在说杜鹃鸟这种孵卵寄生习性。杜甫的解释是中国古代的一个传说，杜鹃鸟是蜀国早期一个君主变身。扬雄的《蜀王本纪》中记载，杜宇从天而降，到了朱提（今云南省昭通市）。而一个叫“利”的女子，从江源（今四川省崇州市）的井中冒出来。杜宇娶利为妻，在蜀地称王，将国都定在郫（今四川省郫县）。这差不多是商周之际或者春秋时代。虽然杜宇善于农耕，但是不擅于治水，于是让他的宰相鳖灵，治理岷江的洪水。而杜宇趁隙与鳖灵的妻子私通，后来于心有愧，将王位禅让给鳖灵，隐居于岷山。故此传说杜宇死后，每逢农历三月，便化为杜鹃，以叫声催促蜀人趁农时播种。另外一个说法认为杜宇实际上是被鳖灵推翻后逃亡，因复位不成，死后怨魂化为杜鹃。

无论如何，杜宇是蜀国的君王，因此做了杜鹃鸟，也有特权，让其他鸟为他哺雏。塔拉雀本来是杜鹃的好朋友，但是杜鹃鸟杀熟，故意混入塔拉雀的鸟巢，吃掉塔拉雀的蛋，然后狸猫换太子，孵卵寄生。而塔拉雀去上诉，得到了貌似公平的处置，根据生物遗传特征断定后代。很可能所有人都知道这不公平，但是如果根据法律和科学，塔拉雀只能屈从于这样的判决。因此，需要对于科学抱有某种谨慎。如果不知道布谷鸟的孵卵寄生的社会行为，就根据分子生物学进行裁决，很可能是错误的。

Cuckoo and Tara Bird

In the Achang area, there is a saying that cuckoo lays eggs, while tara bird hatches eggs in vain. It turned out that cuckoo and tara bird had been good friends. Cuckoo was lazy and could not build a house well. Tara bird often invited cuckoo to play in her own house.

Spring was here and the birds were busy breeding off springs. Tara also laid eggs and was busy hatching eggs in her nest. Only cuckoo, still flying here and wandering there, screaming: “Gege, (which means “brother” in Chinese) Gege...”

One day, cuckoo went to tara’s house to play. Tara bird said to cuckoo: “Sister, you should build a house. Don’t play out all day. Otherwise, when the nephews and nieces are born, there will be no home to live in.”

Cuckoo smiled slightly when she heard the words of the tara bird, but she didn’t take them seriously. After a while, cuckoo flew into the forest again and shouted, “Gege, Gege ...” Tara bird listened and shook her head helplessly.

When the sun has risen about ten feet high, the tara bird went out for some business. When the cuckoo saw it, she quietly slipped into the nest of tara, ate a few eggs of tara bird, laid her eggs in the nest of tara bird, and then slipped away.

Because both cuckoo’s and tara’s eggs were emerald green, tara didn’t notice that cuckoo had laid eggs in her nest. Tara nestled the eggs and hatched them, day and night. Finally, the red babies were born. After the birth of the baby birds, tara became busy again in looking for food for the babies.

One day passed; two days passed; ten days and half a month passed, and the babies grew fine soft feather. A month later, the feather of the babies became full, and they started to learn to fly with their mother.

Cuckoo saw that her children had grown up and wanted to get them back, but she was embarrassed to request of tara bird. She frowned, and came up with a great idea, “yes! Go to the King of Birds to complain.” The King of Birds heard cuckoo’s accusation and sent troops to bring the Tara bird into the palace. The Bird King asked, “Tara bird, how can you do this, and grab the kid birds of cuckoo!”

Hearing this, tara brid had no clue of what had happend. She defended herself to the King of Birds: “King, I haven’t grabbed her babies. They are obviously my own babies!”

“Bring the cuckoo!” The King of Birds ordered.

Several guards brought the Cuckoo to the Bird King. “Cuckoo, why are you arguing that the tara bird has snatched your babies?” The King of Birds asked.

Cuckoo turned her face against her friend and said angrily, “King, the Tara bird really grabbed my babies.”

Tara bird glanced at cuckoo and said angrily, “Please speak to your conscience, who has snatched your babies? Don’t blame the good guys!”

“King, I’m telling the truth. The tara bird has snatched my babies. I beg you to speak for me.” Cuckoo knelt in front of the Bird King, pretending to be very sad.

The King of Birds couldn’t break the case, so he sent troops to the tara’s nest, bringing all the babies in the tara’s nest into the palace, and stood in line in the hall, calling cuckoo and tara in front of them.

“Now let me settle the case. Everyone looks closely at these little tits. Those looking like cuckoo are cuckoo’s babies. Those looking like tara bird are tard bird’s babies. There shouldn’t be much more to argue for now.” Announced the King.

Result: Among the four little tits, there were three like cuckoo birds and only one like tara. Cuckoo proudly led the three baby cuckoo away. Only then did the tara bird understand. She scolded fiercely: “Shameless!”

Since then, the tara bird and cuckoo have formed a grudge. As soon as a tara bird sees a cuckoo, she will shout to her partners, “Zheyou (which means “they are here” in Chinese), Zheyou...” When the partners hear the shout, they will quickly fly out of the nest to chase cuckoo.

热乎乎雀

很久以前，有两个伙伴，上山砍柴，下河摸鱼，形影相随，早晚不离。有一天，两人相约去远处做手艺活。伙伴甲背着一卷行李，伙伴乙背着一筒帕米。他俩脚穿草鞋，晓行夜宿，困倦了，就在路边的草棚睡觉；饿了，就淘米装进竹筒，烧熟了吃。他们经过许多村寨，都没有找着活计，只好向远些的地方走去。一天，他们经过一片茂密的树林，小路弯弯，摸去拐来，结果迷了路。天晚了，仍然没有走到有人家的寨子。这时，伙伴乙的米袋里，仅剩下一小撮米了。那点米，别说是两个人吃，一个人也只够熬稀饭。

夜幕笼罩，周围一片迷迷蒙蒙，俩伙伴来到一棵大树下，准备过夜。伙伴乙捏捏筒帕，心想，今晚吃不饱饭，明天再找不着人家，不是就要饿死了吗？于是，伙伴乙便起了心。他对甲说："今晚米也没有了，饿一顿吧。你去树杈上搭好铺睡觉，我在树脚烤火；天亮，我叫你。"

伙伴乙等伙伴甲睡后，就悄悄地把那撮米煮吃了。肚子是饱了，可是火烤胸前暖，风吹背后寒，看了搭在树杈上的铺，又挤不下，只好蹲在火塘边打瞌睡，一边学雀鸟哼着"饱嘟嘟！饱嘟嘟！"伙伴甲睡在被窝里，饥肠叫个咕噜不停，又听到"饱嘟嘟"的叫声，更是忍不住口水淌；又无法，只好嘴里念着"饱吃不及饿睡"，慢慢合上了眼皮。

清早，伙伴甲一觉酣睡醒来，四周寂静无声，只觉全身热乎乎的，情不自禁地哼起"热乎乎！热乎乎！"来。伙伴甲哼了一阵，竖耳一听，似乎远处山坳里也有雀鸟"饱嘟嘟！"的叫声，一声比一声小，越叫越远。他起身到树脚一看，伙伴乙已经冻死了。

伙伴甲十分伤心，他拣些树枝，捋些叶子，把伙伴乙的尸体掩盖好。他再无心往前走了，可是，在折转回家的路上，由于饥饿疲乏，劳累受寒，还没到家，就死在途中了。伙伴甲死后，变成一只小雀，一到清晨就飞到寨边树林里，"热乎乎！热乎乎！"地叫着，飞去飞来，到处呼喊。可惜它的伙伴于心有愧，始终没有回音。

讲述：梁其显

搜集整理：杨叶生

编者按：再好的伙伴，在生存的威胁面前，都是不堪一击的。两个伙伴，如果可以分享食物和温暖，也许不会都死。但是由于一个人的贪心和自私，导致自己冻死，伙伴饿死。变成了雀鸟，一个叫“热乎乎”，一个叫“饱嘟嘟”。听在人们的耳中，提醒谨慎交友，也强调患难与共。实际上，在危及生命的生存战争中，互利才能共赢。利他是人类社会最重要的行为。

Hot Finches

A long time ago, there were two inseparable partners who went up mountains to cut firewood and went down to the rivers to get fish. One day, the two met for work a distance away. Buddy A carried a roll of luggage, and Buddy B carried a barrel of rice. The two wore straw shoes, walking in the day time and camping in the grass shed on the roadside at night. When they were hungry, they put rice in a bamboo tube and cooked it. Though passing through many villages, they could not get any work to do so they had to go farther away. One day, they passed through a dense forest, and the path was twisted and had many turns, thus they got lost. When it was getting late, they were still not able to find any village. At this time, only a handful of rice remained in the rice bag of Buddy B. That rice, can only be cooked as porridge for one person, let alone feeding two hungry buddies.

The night was near and there was a haze around them. The two partners came under a big tree and prepared to spend the night. Buddy B squeezed the rice and thought, "If I can't eat enough tonight and we won't be able to find someone tomorrow, I'm going to starve to death!" So, Buddy B got up. He said to A, "Tonight, there is no more rice for both of us. Let's just fast for one night. You go to get some tree branches to lay a bed and sleep. I will light and watch the fire at the foot of the tree. At dawn, I will call you."

After Buddy A slept, Buddy B quietly cooked the last portion of rice. His belly was full, but the fire roasted his chest warm and the wind blew his back cold. He looked at the bed that Buddy A made which was not enough for two people, so he had no choice but to squat by the fire dozing while imitating a bird humming "Bao Dudu (which means "I am full" in Chinese)! Bao Dudu!" Buddy A slept in the bed, hungry and groaning, and heard the "Bao Dudu" cry, but couldn't help drooling; he could do nothing but to say, "To be full is not as good as a sleep with empty stomach." Slowly he closed his eyelids.

Early next morning, Buddy A woke up and surrounded by silence. He only felt his whole body warmed up. He could not help humming "Re Huhu (which means "warm" in Chinese)! Re Huhu!" Buddy A hummed for a while, and then listened carefully to some bird sound from afar. It seemed that there was a bird's cry of "Bao Dudu!" The sound was getting weaker and weaker and seemed to be moving further away. He stood up and looked at the foot of the tree. Buddy B was already frozen to death.

Buddy A was very sad. He picked some branches and pressed some leaves to cover Buddy B's body. He didn't want to go on anymore, but started on the way back home, due to hunger, tiredness, and fatigue, he died before he arrived at home. After Buddy A died, he became a sparrow, and flew into the woods by the wall in the early morning. "Re Huhu! Re Huhu!" He cried, flew around, and shouted everywhere. It's a pity that his partner felt ashamed and never echoed back.

螺蛳和兔子赛跑

很早以前，有只兔子，在山坡上觅食。它吃饱后，抬起前脚，翘首远望，只见远处一片亮汪汪的。兔子感到新奇，以为那儿会有什么好吃好玩的，很想去逛逛，溜达溜达。于是，兔子连蹿带蹦，来到了坝子的水田边。

兔子是陆地动物，怕下水。兔子在埂子上颠来簸去，东张西望，什么也瞧不着，只见田螺在水里一扭一扭地蠕动。兔子瞄着螺蛳那蠢笨的样子，不禁嘻嘻哈哈地笑起来。螺蛳见长耳朵在埂上发笑，就问："你笑什么？"兔子挤挤眼睛回答："笑你半天三日才走动一丁点。"螺蛳毫不客气地挑战："别看你有四条毛腿，说不定还跑不赢我呢！"兔子一听，好大的口气，忍不住耸耸肩头怪嚷起来："螺蛳啊，你真是不自量力，还是撒泡尿照照你自己吧！"螺蛳一点也不甘示弱："不信，你明天来比一比。"兔子蛮有把握地说："你赢了，我从今不到你田边；你输了，搬到干坡草蓬下晾着。"螺蛳说："那就一言为定"。

当晚，满坝子的螺蛳相互通了气，商量了对策，第二天要和兔子比赛。

兔子也守信用，按时来到田头，它昂着头向田里叫一声："螺蛳！"田里的螺蛳立即答应："喔！"兔子蹶起后脚，一溜烟跑到田尾，连忙喊一声："螺蛳！"田尾的螺蛳马上答应："喔！"兔子追到上丘田叫，螺蛳照常答应："喔！"兔子撵到下丘田喊，螺蛳依然答应："喔！"

兔子本来性急，跑得太快，结果是比输了不说，倒反把前脚都跑短了一截。所以，他们的后代都是前脚比后脚短些，上坡跑得快，下坡打跌滚。以后，凡是有螺蛳的地方，兔子都不去。农民为了防止狡黠的兔子偷吃地里的庄稼，常常串些螺蛳壳挂在地边。兔子看到螺蛳壳，就再也不到那块地来偷吃东西了。

搜集整理：杨叶生

编者按：到处坑蒙拐骗的兔子也有上当受骗的时候！欺骗了兔子的，是更微不足道的螺蛳。打赌，是动物故事里经常出现的场景，赌局的胜负，可以解释一些现象。虽然现在很可以用动物生态学去解释同样的现象，但是这些科学的解释，远没有这些动物故事的解释更动人，也更有启示作用。

兔子在嘲笑别人之后，想凭借自己跑得快的优势，取得对田螺的胜利。但是螺蛳串通一气，用替身的方法，不那么光彩地赢得了比赛。比赛造成了兔子前脚短后腿长，也让农夫用螺蛳来防兔子。

Snail and Rabbit Race

A long time ago, there was a rabbit looking for food on the hillside. After he was full, he lifted his front feet and looked up, and saw a bright place in the distance. The rabbit felt excited, thinking that there would be something delicious and fun there, and wanted to go strolling and strolling. So, the rabbit jumped to the paddy field of the dam.

Rabbits are dry mountain animals and are afraid of going into the water. The rabbit bumped up and down on the ridge, looking around but found nothing, only a snail wriggling in the water. The rabbit looked at the snail's stupid look and couldn't help laughing. Seeing the long ears laughing on the ridge, the snail asked, "What are you laughing at?" "I am laughing that for three days and a half you can only move a little bit." The snail challenged politely, "Don't you see that you have four hairy legs. Maybe you won't beat me even if you run!" The rabbit thought that it was weird, asked and groaned with shaking shoulders, "Snails, you are being over-confident, so pour your own urine and take a look of yourself!" The snail was reluctant to show weakness at all, "If you don't believe it, we can have a race tomorrow." The rabbit said with confidence, "If you win, I will not be at the edge of your field now; If you lose, I will move to dry slope under the straw shed." The snail said, "Then everything is settled."

That night, all the snails gathered with each other and discussed the countermeasures. They had to compete with the rabbit the next day.

The rabbit also kept his word and came to the fields on time. He raised his head and shouted to the field, "Snail!" The snail in the field immediately replied: "Oh!" The rabbit dug with his claws and ran to the end of the field, quickly shouting, "Snail!" The snail in the field immediately answered, "Oh!" The rabbit raced to the top of the field mound, and the snail still replied as usual, "Oh!" The rabbit yelled from the bottom of the mound, and the snail still echoed, "Oh!"

The rabbit was originally short-tempered and ran too fast; however, he not only lost the race but his forefeet became shorter due to the fast run. Therefore, their descendants are shorter in their forefeet than their hind feet, running fast uphill, while rolling downhill. Nowadays, rabbits will not go wherever there are snails. In order to prevent sly rabbits from stealing crops in the field, farmers often string some snail shells hanging on the field. When the rabbits see the shells of the snails, they never come to the field to steal anything.

黄鳝告状

黄鳝在农民的田里到处打洞，农民见了，把黄鳝从洞里抠出来就打。黄鳝很生气，和农民吵了起来。黄鳝说农民不讲理、霸道；农民讲黄鳝坑人。真是公说公有理，婆说婆有理，一个说不服一个。

黄鳝认为自己被打，理在自己一边，就跑到官府里告状。官府听了黄鳝的诉说，派人把农民传进官府。

黄鳝和农民走进公堂后，判官问黄鳝：

“你为哪样要告农民的状？”

黄鳝说：

“我在田中住，

一不逗骚、二不惹祸，农民拿着我，把我的脑壳掼破。”

判官又问农民：“你为哪样这么对待黄鳝？”

农民气愤地说：

“它头像凤凰，尾像枪，拱倒我的田埂，压死我的绿秧。”黄鳝听到这里自觉理亏，趁判官不注意，悄悄地溜走了。从此以后，农民在田里一见到黄鳝，抓住它的尾巴就在田埂上掼它的头。

搜集整理：赵洪顺

编者按：黄鳝是原告，农夫是被告。黄鳝认为农夫不应该打黄鳝，农夫认为应该打。如果黄鳝曾经看过这本书，听到所有涉及人的动物故事，动物基本上都没有好下场，就应该知道，人才是动物中最恶的存在。人类为了自己的生存，开荒种地，挤压了其他动物的生存空间。黄鳝想在人的田里谋食，却成为人的食物。

不过，把人当成一种动物，不过是一个生态系统中的一种存在。动物可以说话，可以起诉人类，还可以找到让人与黄鳝对簿公堂的地方，可见人也没有高明到哪里去。

The Sue from Ricefield Eel

Rice-field eels dug holes in farmers' fields. When farmers saw them, they pick them out of their holes and beat them up. The rice-field eels were angry at the farmers and they began to argue. The rice-field eels said that the farmers were rude and bossy. A farmer said that rice-field eels only entrapped man. It was just like the husband had a reason and the wife had another reason. They continued to argue, but neither of them could convince the other.

The rice-field eel felt that he had been hit and thought he was the victim so he went to the authority to sue the farmers. The authority heard what the rice-field eel proposed and told his minions to get the farmer.

The rice-field eel and the farmer went to the court and the judge asked the rice-field eel,

"Why do you want to sue this farmer?"

The rice-field eel answered,

"I live on the farm. First, I did not goof around; second I did not do bad things. But the farmer held me and hit my head."

Then the judge asked the farmer, " Why did you do this to the rice-field eel?"

The farmer said angrily,

"His head is like a phoenix and tail like a sword. He moved under my field and killed my plants." When the rice-field eel heard this, he felt a little ashamed and wrong about his own opinion. Before the judge paid any attention to him, he simply slipped away. From that day on, when farmers see a rice-field eel in their fields, they will pick it up and break its head.

查九鹊向乌鸦讨工钱

很早以前，查九鹊和乌鸦本来是相好的玄衣朋友，后来却成了冤家对头。查九鹊见了乌鸦就要讨工钱，三言两语不对头，不是吵就是打，总没有和睦的时候。传说，这当中还有一个故事呢。

有一次，乌鸦要出远门串亲戚，可是窝里毛茸茸的幼儿，翅膀还没有翎毛，要飞也飞不动。乌鸦思来想去，没有更好的办法，就想把幼儿放给查九鹊照管几天，回来付给工钱。

于是，乌鸦找到了查九鹊，说：

“朋友，我要去出远门，请你代我照管几天窝里的儿女。”

查九鹊素来精明能干，想到给乌鸦守儿看女，要耽误工夫，要花费吃灶，人亲财不亲，得把工钱讲断，好话说在前，丑事做朝后。便说：

“朋友，得的，只是每天得开给我三钱银子的工价。”

“好说，照常论价，每天三钱银子，只消四天工夫，回来一两二钱银子，保你分文不爽。”乌鸦也干脆利落。

乌鸦是毛黑，骨头黑，心也黑。回来见着查九鹊，伸手摸摸口袋里的银子，心里怪舍不得，就想打赖账。它左捞右捞，好歹掂出三钱银子递给查九鹊，嘴里甜言蜜语，说：

“哎，朋友！我出门破费大，眼下不恰好，隔几天，我给你送来。你别多心。”

查九鹊接过三钱碎银，也不见怪，客客气气地说声：“隔两天再给，没关系。”

可是，日出日落，十天半月不见乌鸦来给工钱；又过了半打半年，依然不见乌鸦来还工钱。查九鹊觉得乌鸦不守信用，便出门去寻找乌鸦讨工钱。乌鸦不是不见查九鹊，见的，山不转路转，天再大，地再宽，总有相逢的时日。可是乌鸦心疼那九钱银子，一见查九鹊的影子，就忙不迭地躲；从空中飞进密竹林，从树枝头缩进树叶底下，从房头梭下屋檐脚，给查九鹊找它找得好费心神。

有一天，查九鹊和乌鸦窄路相逢，乌鸦再也无法遁迹，只好硬着头皮打招呼。查九鹊这回也就明话直说，可不讲情面了，便开口说：

“朋友，你害得我好找，工钱八九钱，给过来。”

乌鸦哪舍得银子，便扮出记不起的样子，就“啊，啊……”地嚷着要逃走。查九鹊也不饶它，死死盯着它，直喊：“八九钱，八九钱……”乌鸦急急飞，查九鹊紧紧追，最后竟然打起来了。查九鹊虽小，却占着它有理，理直气壮；乌鸦理屈心虚，往往只有招架之功，没有还手之力。直到如今，查九鹊一见乌鸦，总是追着它讨工钱，连声喊叫：“八九钱，八九钱……”

讲述：杨从根

搜集整理：杨叶生　孙加申

编者按：最终成了冤家对头的，很多都是从好朋友开始的。这对朋友，因为需要帮乌鸦带孩子，先是说定了工钱，后来乌鸦赖账，查九鹊追账，不可开交。可能孩子们没有借钱给人的经验，某种意义上，借钱给那些不还的人，是一个人成长经验中的一部分，从此学会了在钱财上的谨慎。莎士比亚在他的名著《哈姆雷特》中有一句经典的对白：“不要向别人借钱也不要借给别人钱，向别人借钱会丧失尊严，借给别人钱会人财两空”。

Chajiu Bird Asked Wages from a Raven

Long ago, Chajiu birds and ravens were good friends, but in the end, they became enemies. When a Chajiu bird saw a raven, he asked for his wages and could never get it right. With no more than three words they would fight each other. They never had peace with each other. There is a legend about it.

Once upon a time, there was a raven wanting to go out to visit a relative. But in his nest were new born baby ravens. They had no feathers on their wings yet so they could not fly. There was no way to take them, the raven thought for a long time but still no answer came. So, he thought of having the Chajiu bird baby-sit his kids for the time being. When he got back, he would pay the wages.

So, the raven found Chajiu bird and said,

"Friend, I'm going far away. Please take care of my children in the nest for a few days."

Chajiu bird had always been shrewd and capable. He thought that if he helped raven, it would cost both time and money, so he had to make it clear about the payment. "Saying ugly sentences first, doing good things backward". Therefore, he said:

"My friend, it's fine for me to help you, but you just have to pay me three Qian per day."

"That's no problem. It's reasonable to get paid. Three Qian silver per day and only four days of work till I come back. That would be one Liang and two Qian silver. I will pay you all clear." The raven was also neat.

The feather of the raven is black, the bone of the raven is black, and the heart of the raven is also black. When he got back, he went to see the Chajiu bird and reached to his pockets to pay the wages. But he did not want to give it but to be delinquent. He searched all over his pockets, pulled out three Qian silver to Chajiu bird and said in a sweet voice:

"Ah, dear friend! I spent a lot of money when I went out. Can you wait for a few days and I'll pay you all the rest wage? Trust me."

Chajiu bird took the money and was not suspicious, "You can pay me in two days. It's okay."

However, sunrise and sunset, there was no raven coming for almost half a month. More time passed by, the raven still didn't pay back the wages. Chajiu bird felt that the raven did not keep his word, so he went out to look for the raven to get his money back. There was no way for the raven to escape from the Chajiu bird forever. If the mountains not moving, rivers would. No matter how big the world was, there was eventually a time for them to meet. But the raven was distressed at paying the nine Qian silver. As soon as he saw the shadow of Chajiu bird, he hid in a hurry. He flew into the dense bamboo forest from the sky, hid from the branches to the leaves, and shuttled from the front to the back corner of the house. It was really difficult and a great effort for the Chajiu bird to get him.

One day, Chajiu bird met the raven on a narrow road, and the raven could no longer escape, so he had to greet the Chajiu bird. The Chajiu said straight forwardly this time, not hesitating about losing the friendship.

"Friend, suffered from trying to find you. You owed me nine Qian silver. Give the money to me here."

The raven for sure did not want to hand over the money. He pretended that he did not remember. "Ah, ah, ah", he cried and got ready to escape. But the Chajiu bird didn't let him go and stared at the him "Ba-Jiu-Qian (which means eight or nine Qian silver in Chinese! Ba-Jiu-Qian..." The raven flew in a hurry. Chajiu bird followed closely, and finally they fought. Chajiu was small, but he was the victim and straightforward. The raven was frisky knowing that he was wrong having only the power to fight off but did not have the strength to fight back. Till now, when the Chajiu birds see the ravens, they always chase them for wages and shout: "Ba-Jiu-Qian ..."

公鸡喝水要抬头张望天空

很古的时候，公鸡和麻雀是亲密的伙伴。它们虽然不是同族，却比同族还亲。它们个头儿大小不一，却不互相嫌弃欺侮。平时你来我往，互通有无，无话不谈。可是世间之事，恩去怨来，得失一瞬间。现在人们仍然看见，公鸡饮水的时候，呷上一口水后，总要抬起头来，张望一下天空，而且要伸缩一下脖颈，才能把水喝下去。为什么呢？前人留下了一个动人的传说：

有一次，麻雀到公鸡家里玩耍，两个叽叽咕咕地交谈了一阵，上谈天文地理，下谈鸡毛蒜皮。谈天论地，觉得疲乏了，公鸡便建议到山林里去走一趟，换换空气，看看景致，逍遥一番。麻雀听了正中下怀，欣然乐意。

公鸡和麻雀连飞带跑，一会儿跳，一会儿摆，耍得痛快淋漓，只是天热干燥，它们都感到有点饥渴。麻雀便提议，到山坳里找点水喝，捉几只蛆虫充饥，啄上几个浆果填填肚子。公鸡听了点头同意。

公鸡在地上跑，专门寻觅蚁虫作美餐，麻雀在树枝上飞，专门觅食熟果作佳肴。不一会儿，都填满了饥肠，就是觉得口干舌燥，想痛痛快快地喝上几口凉水。它们转了几个山坳，都不见清泉流水，公鸡觉得嗓子干得要冒火星，便急不可待指着一塘潮湿的坳坑，对麻雀说："你看这地下一定有水，你扒开泥土，水就会淌出来。"

麻雀歪歪脑袋，晓得公鸡想偷懒，图享现成便宜，便回答：

"你身大脚长，嘴尖爪利，还是你扒吧。"

公鸡垂着脑袋，装出有气无力的神态，对麻雀说：

"哎，我现在乏得很，你个小机灵，我伸开翅膀替你遮荫，你先扒吧！"

麻雀也不再想推辞，吃亏人常常在，扒就扒吧。于是麻雀左右开弓，左脚抠土，右脚扒泥，终于扒开了一个洞穴，只见泉水从地下冒出来。麻雀把泥坑扒成一个小井，泉水流满了小井，一会儿就澄清了。麻雀眼看清汪汪的泉水，挖洞累得满头大汗，正想伏下身子，来它个喝饱饮足，公鸡却突然吼叫起来：

"慢着，先老后幼，从大到小，轮着来；我先喝了，你再喝。"

麻雀知道公鸡恃强凌弱，仗势欺人，十分气愤，可看看公鸡那个头，

自己不是对手，评讲道理又无人帮腔，只好移动身子，让公鸡先喝水。

公鸡伸长脖子，正向水井里点去，麻雀灵机一动，就在这一刹那间，想出了一个捉弄公鸡的点子。公鸡刚把水含到嘴里，麻雀突然尖声叫起来：

“嗨！公鸡大哥，雷公要打你了！”

公鸡吓得来不及把水咽下，赶忙抬头望天空，不见雷公，更没有雷母，才把含在嘴里的水慢慢咽下。可是，这一恐吓，却给公鸡吓成了一辈子改不掉的老毛病：公鸡喝水的时候，总要含着水抬头望着天空，才能把水咽下肚去。

讲述：孙加金

搜集整理：孙加申

编者按：人在做，天在看。麻雀虽小，却不肯吃亏。和公鸡前面有多要好，后来就有多别扭。的确公鸡想占便宜在先，而且恃强凌弱，仗势欺人，十分过分。现实生活中，这样的人很多，弱小者往往和麻雀一样，求天无门。他们只能用雷公这样的神明来吓唬这些欺软怕硬的坏人。

Why the Rooster Looks up at the Sky When Drinking Water

In ancient times, roosters and sparrows were close friends. Although they were not of the same race, they were closer than those of the same race. They were of different sizes, but they did not dislike and bully each other. Usually they visited each other, each making up what the other lacked and having nothing they could not share with each other. But in this world, there is always a gain and lost as well as love and hatred. Now it can still be found that when the rooster drinks water, after taking a sip, he has to raise his head, looking at the sky, and stretches his neck to drink the water. Why? The predecessors left a moving legend.

Once, a sparrow went to a rooster's house to play, and the two chatted for a while, talking about heaven and earth, big and small. After they were tired of chatting, the rooster suggested going to the forest to change their environment, look at the scenery, and relax. It was also what the sparrow was thinking of, so he happily agreed with him.

The rooster and the sparrow flew in a row, hopping and swinging occasionally. They had a goodtime and felt very happy, but it was hot and dry. The sparrow proposed to find some water in the mountain pool, to catch a few maggots to eat, and to peck a few berries to fill the stomach. The rooster nodded and agreed.

The rooster ran around on the ground, looking for ants and insects for meal, and the sparrow flew on the branches, foraging for ripe fruits for delicacies. After a while, they were both getting full, but were thirsty and wanted to drink a few sips of cold water. They turned around a few hollows, but they didn't see the clear spring water. The rooster felt that his throat was going to be sparking, and he could not wait to point to a pool of damp pool and said to the sparrow: "You see there must be water under the ground. Dig the soil and the water will flow out."

The sparrow crooked its head, knowing that the rooster wanted to be lazy.

"You have big feet and sharp claws, so you should dig it."

The rooster lowered his head, pretending to be weak, and said to the sparrow:

"Hey, I'm so tired now. You're a clever man. I'll stretch out my wings to shade you. Please dig it first!"

The sparrow was tired of finding excuses. After all, some one had to suffer. So, he just started digging. The sparrow dug the soil from side to side, left to right, and finally made a hole. Water did spring out! The sparrow then plucked the mud pit into a small well so that the spring water filled the small well. It was clarified in a moment. The sparrow saw the cool spring water, digging a hole and sweating tiredly, and was about to bow down to drink it, then the rooster suddenly roared:

"Slow down, the old first and then the young. From big to small, come in turns; I drink first, and then you drink."

The sparrow knew that the rooster was trying to bully him, and got very angry. But looking at the big rooster's head, he could not be an opponent. He had reasons but no helper at all. Therefore, he had to move his body and let the rooster drink first.

The rooster stretched his neck and was pointing his mouth towards the well. Just at that time, the sparrow came up with a trick to play on the rooster. When the rooster just put water in his mouth, the sparrow suddenly screamed:

"Hi! Brother rooster, the Lord of Thunder is going to strike you!"

The rooster was too scared to swallow the water, and quickly looked up at the sky, without seeing the Lord of Thunder nor the Madam of Thunder, he slowly swallowed the water in his mouth. However, this intimidation scared the rooster into an illness that could not be cured of a lifetime: when the rooster drinks water, he must always look up at the sky with water before he can swallow it.

蚂蚱和猴子打架

很古老的时候，开天辟地的始祖遮帕麻和遮咪麻，给各种动物分封疆域。猴子生性机灵，爬高上矮，谁也比不过它；偷抢摸窃，谁也拿它无法。只有它占便宜，没有它吃亏的时候。因为猴子遭到大家的一致非议，不得人心，结果就被发配到箐窠里生活，靠采撷野果充饥果腹。有一年秋收时节，猴子感到在山林里生活，有点腻烦，落叶萧萧，熟果渐少，看到坝子里谷穗摇曳，一片黄灿灿，很想下山去霸占一块地盘。

猴子三蹿两跳，跑到田边，抬头四顾：天高地阔，比起在山林里，既宽敞又明亮。猴子伸手掐了几穗黄谷，蹲在埂上剥米粒，放到嘴里嚼嚼，米浆甜滋滋的，比山毛野果，要润口得多。猴子正在剥米粒的当儿，一群蚂蚱从田里飞过来，看见猴子坐在田塍上吃米粒，气愤填膺。蚂蚱们叽叽喳喳议论开了，有的说："猴子来了，可不妙，糟蹋了谷穗，主人可要怪罪我们啰！"有的说："猴子是黄毛长脸，得一望二，不把它赶走，地盘被它占领，我们就无家可归了。"经过一番商讨，确定了轰走猴子的办法。

蚂蚱问猴子："你跑到我们地方干什么？"猴子听了，扮了一副鬼脸："哟，小小蚂蚱，竟敢质问我。小心我把你们一个个掐了吃掉。"蚂蚱一点不胆怯："别看你长得像黄狗黑羊，打赢我们，就准你到田里吃谷穗；打不赢，就回你山上去。"猴子说："好！看着我把你们踩成肉酱！"蚂蚱喊道："明天太阳当顶，领着你的猴儿们，扛着棍棒来。"

第二天正午，一群猴子扛着棍棒来了。蚂蚱早站在谷棵上，翅膀已被太阳晒得硬铮铮的了。猴子不见蚂蚱，更加趾高气扬，摆出一副不可一世的架势，吼着："蚂蚱们，都钻到你祖祖的尿罐里去了，给我乖乖地飞远些吧！"说时迟，那时快，蚂蚱听见猴子乍呼，从四面八方一齐飞来，叮在猴子的脑门上。猴子看见蚂蚱落在头上，就舞起棍棒互相敲。蚂蚱待棍子打来，又闪身飞起。棍子正好落在猴子的头上。蚂蚱飞起又飞落，结果，猴子敲来敲去，都打在伙伴的头上，一个个被打得鼻青脸肿。猴子气得吹胡子瞪眼，没有办法，纷纷丢了棍棒，抚着疼痛不止的脑袋，跑上山去了。

搜集整理：孙加申

编者按：开篇讲猴子的机灵和鬼道，喜好占便宜，绝不吃亏。我们身边都有这样不讨喜的人，让大家敬而远之。猴子也因此被驱逐到深山老林，那里没有充足的食物和安全的房子。蚂蚱看到猴子偷吃人类的粮食，气愤填膺，想到的也是自己被怪罪，自己的地盘被侵蚀，所以也是害虫的思维。

两害相权取其轻，猴子和蚂蚱进行了一场较量，有趾高气扬，有耀武扬威，先是舌枪唇战，后是棍棒相加。这样的约架方式，是人类经常采用的次序。蚂蚱利用自己的身量小，作为优势，和体量大的猴子进行搏斗，实际是猴子自己攻击自己。这属于詹姆斯·C. 斯科特所著《弱者的武器》里所描述的那种斗争方式。可能在城里人看来，这就是一种诡诈，但是在西南山地，这是一种生存策略。

The Fight Between Grasshoppers and Monkeys

A long time ago, the creators of the world Zhe Pama and Zhe Mima gave all kinds of animals their own realm. Monkeys were clever. They could climb any kind of trees, and no other animals could compare with them. They stole things but no one knew what to do about it. They would gain extra advantage rather than suffer loss. Because of this, the monkeys were unanimously unpopular, and they were sent to live in valleys and only the wild fruits were found to satisfy their hunger. That year, during the autumn harvest season, the monkeys felt a bit bored living in the mountain forest. The leaves were falling and the ripe fruits were falling also. Seeing the wheat swaying on the fields, yielding and golden, they really wanted to go down there to live.

The monkeys jumped and ran to the field. They looked up the sky, which was much brighter and wider than it was in the valley. They picked grain and chowed it. The juice was sweet and smooth, although not more tasteful than the wild fruits in the forest. When the monkeys were pilling the grains, a swarm of grasshoppers came to the field and saw the monkeys eating the grains. They were really angry and talked to one another. Some said, "Monkeys are here. That is not good. They ruined our field, so our master will be mad at us!" Some said, "The monkeys are cheeky and greedy. If we don't chase them away, they will take our place and then we won't have a place to stay." After discussing for a long time, they finalized a way to drive the monkeys away.

A grasshopper asked one monkey, "What are you doing here?" When the monkey heard this, he made a face at him and answered, "Hey, little grasshopper. You dare ask me? Watch out or I will squeeze you to death then eat you." The grasshopper was not afraid, "Don't highly evaluate yourself just because you look much bigger than us. If only you can beat us in a fight, we will let you come down to eat this grain. However, if we win, you must go back to your valley." "Okay! You will see how we kill you all!" The monkey replied. The grasshopper shouted, "Tomorrow when the sun rises, come with your monkey brothers with sticks."

At noon the next day, a group of monkeys came with sticks. The grasshopper had long been standing on the valley tree, and his wings had been hardened by the sun. The monkey did not see the grasshopper, so he stood higher, posing with an incomparable posture, shouting: "Grasshoppers, did you all get into your grandfather's urine tank? I order you quietly fly far away!" Quicker than words can tell, the grasshoppers heard the monkey screaming, flew from all directions and landed on the heads of the monkeys. When the monkeys saw the grasshoppers on others' heads, they waved the sticks in their hands and knocked on one another to kill the grasshoppers. When the grasshoppers saw the sticks coming towards them, they flew up again. The sticks fell on the monkeys' heads. The grasshoppers flew and landed, then landed and flew. As a result, the monkeys only hit each other with sticks. Each of their wounds turning black and blue. The monkeys were foaming with rage. They had no other choice but to drop their sticks, held their painful heads and ran back to the mountain valley.

大蚂蜂的故事

古代，怒江和澜沧江上游流域活动着阿昌等部族的先民古浪峨人。当时那里森林茂密，动物资源极其丰富，古浪峨人过着以狩猎渔牧采集为主兼有原始农业的生活。

传说有对夫妇背着婴儿到地里点种旱谷，顺便到附近的树林砍干柴挑回家，便把睡着的婴儿放在地边的树下。但等他们回到树下，才发现婴儿被飞来的黄蚂蜂叮死了。丈夫很悲伤，要寻到黄蚂蜂的窝，替儿子报仇。他就跟着黄蚂蜂飞去的方向追踪，翻过碧罗雪山，越过无数深沟大箐，来到碧罗江山头一座大悬岩下，终于发现黄蚂蜂窝就在大悬岩上。他就砍来长竹竿用松明柴拴在竹竿头，点燃了一把火，将火把撑到大悬岩上，烧毁了这窝大蚂蜂。从火把落下的火苗，把悬岩下的草地烧了一大片。后来他狩猎路过，看到被火烧过的地十分肥沃，恰巧他身边的箭筒里还有几粒籼米谷，便用木棍戳洞点下。过了一季，他再来到那里看时，发现种下的籼米谷长得很好，结出了沉甸甸的穗子。他知道这里是个好地方，又无人烟，就带着几户族人把家口搬到那里住，后来生子生孙，在那里发达兴旺起来了。

杨叶生录自李道生、李浚采写的资料

编者按：这个故事里面包括了几个重要的话题：刀耕火种，民族迁徙，除害复仇。看似讲的是黄蚂蜂的故事，实际是一部人类的短史。阿昌族是从高原迁徙过来的，之前就是狩猎渔牧采集的游猎民族，经过这个事情，转变成为刀耕火种的游耕民族。报复血仇，这是游猎和游牧群体的核心故事，一旦变为耕种的民族，血仇优先就会退让给生产活动优先了。

刀耕火种在西南地区是更合适当地自然地理条件的生产方式，灌溉一方面不现实，另一方面会造成水土流失和土壤退化。实际上云南历经数千年的刀耕火种，森林覆盖率仍然很高。而在制止了刀耕火种之后，森林覆盖率不升反降，就证明了刀耕火种并非毁坏森林的罪魁祸首。真正破坏森林的，是人的贪得无厌和技术手段无所不用其极。

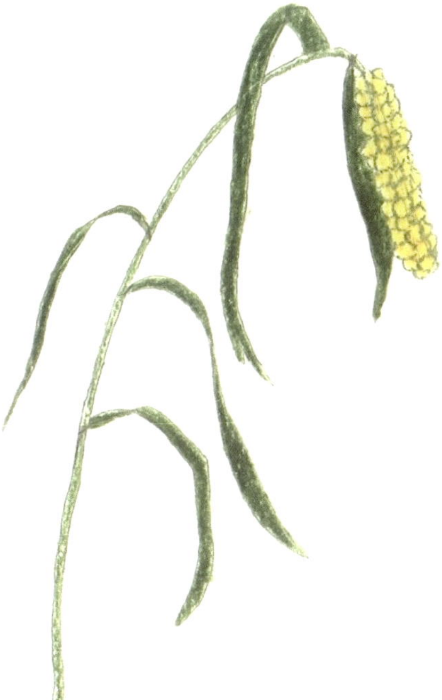

The Story of Wasps

In ancient times, Gulang'e—ancestors of Achang and other tribes were active in the upper reaches of Nu River and Lancang River. In that age, there were forests full of animals. Gulang'e people lived on hunting and fishing. In addition, there was also farming.

Legends say that there was a husband and wife with their children. They went to plant and cut wood for the house to use. They left their sleeping baby under a tree. When they came back, they found out that the baby was stung to death by wasps. The husband was sad and went up to the hill to kill the wasps. He followed the direction where the wasps were flying, climbed over the Biluo Snow Mountain, crossed countless deep ditches, and came to a large overhanging rock at the top of the Biluojiang Mountain. Finally, he found that the wasp's honeycomb was on the large overhanging rock. He cut down a long bamboo pole, tied Songming firewood to the head of the bamboo pole, ignited a fire, propped the torch on the big hanging rock, and burned the nest of big bees. The flames falling from the torch burned a large area of grass under the hanging rock. Later, he hunted by that area and found that the ground burned by the fire was very fertile. It happened that there were still a few grains of Indica rice in his arrow barrel, and he poked it with a wooden stick. One season later, when he came there to see it again, he found that the indicia rice planted had grown very well with heavy ears. He knew that it was a good place, and there were no people. He took several clansmen to move their families there, and they had children and grandchildren. Later they prospered.

树木不走路的传说

据说，从前树木都会走路，把树砍倒后，可以像吆牛马一样赶着回来，而现在树木怎么不走路了呢？我们阿昌族有这样一个传说：

一天，有个妇女上山拿柴，她急着要快点回家给丈夫煮饭，拣得些细柴，捆成一捆，就赶着柴往回走。路上柴像螺蛳一样慢慢腾腾地磨蹭，三步一扭，四步一歇，妇人也只好跟在后面走走停停，停停走走。走到半路，妇人实在挨不得，嫌柴走得太慢，心想还不及把柴背在身上走来得干脆，就埋怨说：“细柴啊，你真是踩死蚂蚁不留种，不如我背你走一段吧！”她取下包头布，把柴套起背着走。

路边的树木看见柴被人背着走，都很新奇，认为这捆柴有福气，走路不费力，往后自己被砍倒了，也尝尝让人背着走的滋味。

柴让人背着走感到很轻松，而且一下就来到了家。柴把这事告诉了邻居，邻居又告诉给树木，传来传去，遍山的树木都晓得了让人背着走十分舒服。

第二天，妇人又上山去砍柴，砍倒一棵树，躺着一棵，动也不动；一连砍了几棵，都睡在地上。妇女人横吆竖赶，就是不走，只好一根一根地扛回家去。从此，树木被砍倒后，再也不走路了。

搜集整理：杨叶茂

编者按：在阿昌族的世界里，万物有灵，都和人一样好奇、羡慕、传言。哪怕是树木，也可以走路，还可以说话，遇到改变的可能时，也尝试新的行为。

从这个故事里，可以看到一次转变，树木从自动的，变为被动的。而且是单向的转变，不可逆转。好像社会中一些变化一样，一旦产生了，就变成了新的常态了。如果不想有改变，那么最好就不要有第一次。

The Legend of Why Trees Don't Walk

It was said that trees were once able to walk. When people cut one down, it would be like a herding sheep. But why have the trees stopped moving? Well, the Achang tribe has a legend.

One day, there was a woman climbing up the hill to get wood. She was anxious to go home with the wood to make some food for her husband. She picked a few thick sticks, bundled the sticks together and herded them back to her house. On her way, the sticks were walking like snails. Every three steps they panted; every four steps they rested. The woman had to follow their steps and went really slowly. Walked then rested; rested then walked. At the half way point, the woman thought that the sticks were going too slow. She thought about carrying them back, and said, "Sticks, when you walk you are afraid of killing the ants. How about I carry you instead!" She took off her head wrap and piggybacked them all the way home.

The other trees and sticks saw this when they passed, and thought that it was cool and new. They thought that those sticks were lucky because they did not need to walk. When they were cut down as well, they stayed in place and let the person carry them so they could also feel what the sticks felt when they were carried.

The wood felt good when the person carried it, and came home at once. They told the neighbor about it, and the neighbor told the trees again and again, and the trees all over the mountain knew that it was very comfortable to ride on people's backs.

The next day, the woman went up the mountain again to cut wood. She cut down a tree and lay it down. It didn't move. After cutting several trees, they slept on the ground. The woman droved and droved, but they did not move. She had to carry them home one by one. Since then, after the trees are cut down, they no longer walk any more.

樱桃疮·花桃·杞木·松树

阿昌人的村头寨尾，无处不有樱桃树。一到十冬腊月，满树樱花，红彤彤的，煞是好看；成群的蜜蜂，绕着樱花，“嗡嗡”地采花酿蜜，颇为热闹。牡丹、芍药一类，红花玉叶，鲜艳悦目；殷勤的蝴蝶，浓施粉黛，为她们翩翩起舞。其他各色花卉，相形见绌。

一天，花王召集群芳议事，樱桃自恃花魁，姗姗来迟。牡丹、芍药来到殿堂，环顾四周，不见樱桃坐堂，一阵窃窃私语后，急忙跪在花王脚下，奏道：“花王陛下，樱桃自诩英伟，目空一切，傲视我等弱花柔草不言，还敢违拗王命，真是大逆不道。望乞严惩不贷，以平小辈胸中怨忿。”花王听了牡丹、芍药的一番谗言，不作审慎，便当堂判道：“且看世间，好马生怪癖，十马九不全，无一完美，让樱桃树皮生疮，虫蛀蚁啃。”自此以后，樱桃树总是一壳一壳的，满身长着黑色的疮包。

一次，树王召集会议，分封疆域。除花桃、杞木树外，各类花草树木，前挤后推，蜂拥着前来讨封。牡丹、芍药、玉兰……深得树王青睐，被封赠在艺苑御园生长；杜鹃、山茶、樱桃、攀枝花……因体魄伟岸、深孚众望，树王对它们疑生信义消，统统被发配在山上。花桃、杞木，身粗个子高，紧走慢跑，还是来迟一步。地盘已经分划完毕，树王无奈，只好叫花桃、杞木到山边陡坡安家落脚。所以，花桃、杞木都是长在贫瘠、陡峭的地方。

人们都晓得，砍了竹子，会有雨后春笋，为它光耀门庭；砍了柳树，还会春风吹又生，一派生机；砍了杞木、花桃，也会春来发几枝，可望十年树木长风烟；而那松树，却是砍一棵完蛋一棵，再也不会分蘖生枝。据说，这还有一个根由呢。

很古以前，树王提着拄棍，到茫茫林海去巡视。山高路陡，轿子抬不上去，滑竿也不好坐，只得一步一步地扶摇而上。走到半山上，浓密的松树，枝叶茂盛，蓬勃兴旺，树王看了，啧啧称赞：“此乃山中奇秀，高楼作柱，虹桥作梁……”树王言罢，想坐下来休息一会，就近拣了一个松树桩，一屁股坐下了。

一阵阵松涛起伏，一股股凉风吹拂，树王感到十分惬意，疲劳尽消。于是，树王理起拄棍，打算继续行走。可是，树王怎么也站不起来，屁股下面好像有什么东西紧紧地黏着；树王头一拱一拱的，咋个也立不起身；树王扶紧拄棍，使劲一挣，只听“嗞”的一声，绸袍被撕破了。树王回头仔细一看，原来松树桩上有许多松脂，再看看背后的绸缎撕烂了好大一块，心中十分气恼，便用拄棍跺着地，口吐咒言：“从今后，松树让它长一棵，砍一棵；砍一棵，完一棵，不准它再发。”所以，松树都是砍了后，根部也就死去，再不会分蘖发枝。

搜集整理：杨叶生　宋甫

编者按：这篇文章，已经超过了一般意义上的口传故事了。无论是遣词造句，还是权力分配，都是一位经历过人世的文人，以树木故事来比喻自己的人生。樱桃姗姗来迟是过错，但是被贬被罚被惩却是让人心生不平，因此作为个体的樱桃在形象和遭遇上，落入尘埃。随后的分封土地，显示出权力的任性和谄媚者的势利，以及粗笨者的不幸。松树本来与世无争，在山腰上自由自在，却因为没有招待好树王，或者说树王自己无知犯错，却惩罚了松树失去了断枝再萌的能力。权力的肆意和霸道可见一斑。

Cherry Sore, Peachblossom, Wolfberry, Pine

There are cherry trees everywhere in the villages of Achang. In the cold twelfth lunar month, the trees are full of cherry blossoms and glowing red, which is really beautiful. There are swarms of bees, around the cherry blossoms, "buzzing" to gather flowers and honey, which is quite lively. Tree-peony and peony are red flowers and jade leaves. They are bright and beautiful, attracting beautiful butterflies to dance for them. Other flowers of all colors are dwarfed by comparison.

One day, the King of Flowers summoned the group to discuss things. The cherry thought herself was the oiran, so she came too late. Tree-peony and peony came to the temple and looked around. They didn't see the cherry sitting in the hall. After a whisper, they hurriedly knelt at the feet of the King of Flowers and said, "Your Majesty, the cherry is proud of herself, and has nothing to look at. She dares to defy the king's order. It's a big injustice. We want to beg for punishment and ease our anger." The King of Flowers listened to the remarks of tree-peony and peony. Without thinking it through, he judged in court, "Looking at the world, good horses have strange ringworm. Nine horses of ten are incomplete, not perfect, so that the cherry's bark is with sores and insects gnaw it." From then on, the cherry tree is always shell by shell, covered with black bags.

Once, *the Tree King* convened a meeting to divide the territory. Except peachblossom and Wolfberry, all kinds of flowers and trees, squeezed forward and pushed back, and flocked to come to discuss the deal. Tree-peony and peony, magnolia ... won the favor of *Tree King*, and were granted to grow in Yiyuan Royal Garden; azaleas, camellia, cherries, Panzhihua... were due to their great body and popular, *the King of Trees* was suspicious of them, They were all rejected and distributed in the mountains. Peachblossom and Wolfberry, who were thick and tall, walked and jogged, came later. The territory had been divided, and the King of the Trees had no choice but to send peachblossom and Wolfberry to settle down on the steep hillside. Therefore, peachblossom and Wolfberry grew in barren and steep places.

Everyone knows that when bamboo is cut, there will be sprouts after a spring rain, and it will grow by the door; when the willow is cut, it will go on growing after spring breezes begin to blow. If the Wolfberry and peachblossom are cut, they will also grow a few branches in spring, which are expected to flourish in ten years. However, If the pine tree is cut, it will no longer grow branches. It is said that there is another reason.

Very long ago, the Tree King carried a stick and went to inspect the boundless forest. The mountain was high and the road was steep, the sedan chair could not be lifted up, and the sliding rod was not easy to sit on. So, the Tree King had to walk step by step. Walking to the middle of the mountain, where there were dense pine trees with lush foliage, flourishing and prosperous, the Tree King saw them, and praised, "This is a wonderful show in the mountain. The tree trunk could be used to serve as a tall building's columns and a rainbow bridge's beam..." After saying this the Tree King wanted to sit down and take a rest. So he picked a pine stump nearby and sat down.

With the waves of pine surging and the breeze blowing, the Tree King felt very comfortable and relaxed. As a result, the Tree King was refreshed and prepared to walk on. However, the King of Trees couldn't stand up, it seemed to be something sticking tightly under his ass. The King of Trees tried hard, but he couldn't stand up, the King of Trees held his stick tightly, earnestly, and only heard sizzling sound, the silk robe was torn. The King of Trees looked back and saw that there was a lot of pine resin on the pine stump. Then he saw that the satin on the back of his robe was torn into a large piece. He was very annoyed, so he stomped on the ground with a stick and spit the curse, "From now on, let the pine tree grow itself. Cut one and one is dead. It is forbidden to branch out again." Therefore, when the pine trees are cut, the roots will die, and they will no longer branch out.

疙瘩竹倒栽的由来

西南地区，依山傍水的寨子边，人们不难看到一蓬蓬青竹。竹节的一方尽是倒长的小枝条，人是无法钻进竹棵中间的，竹节也比其他各种竹子的要大要硬，农村百姓叫作疙瘩竹。栽竹子要刨出一年青的竹根，截下五尺许长，把竹根埋在地下才能活。但栽疙瘩竹，只消截下根部五尺长的一段，要倒着栽在地下，便可活起来。对此，阿昌族民间有如下的说法。

远古的时候，遮帕麻造了天，遮咪麻织了地，又一起创造了人类。后来妖魔腊訇作乱，造了假太阳和假月亮，使世间阴阳颠倒，水族被撵上山，树木竹子被拔起倒立。遮帕麻用斗法战胜腊訇，用毒菌灭了腊訇，射落了假太阳和假月亮，把水族重新赶下水，把倒插的树木重新扶正。但却把倒插的疙瘩竹漏下没有扶正。于是，疙瘩竹就成了今天这种样子，竹节的斜枝倒长，要倒栽才能活。

讲述：梁其美

记录：杨叶生

编者按：世界曾经颠倒，世界曾蒙拯救。人类是活在一次救赎之后的族群，善与恶的大战，仍然没有完结。虽然上一次创造世界的大公地母获得了胜利，但是恶魔只是暂时被击退，仍然可能卷土重来。

疙瘩竹就是那次世界颠倒的记号，让世人铭记现今的秩序来之不易。每个人的每个行为，都会影响这个世界的走向，或者与善一起战胜罪恶，或者堕落作恶。

The Origin of Cypress Bamboo Planted Upside Down

In the south western area, it is not hard for people to find bamboos by the water in a village. A certain knotted bamboo grows upside down and it is really hard for people to go through the bamboo area. The knotted bamboo is harder than other bamboo, so people called it cypress bamboo. If you want to plant this bamboo, you need to find a young bamboo root and cut for five feet and then bury the root in the dirt for it to grow. But for the cypress bamboo, you need to cut the root also five feet and stick it in the dirt upside down so it may live. To explain this, the Achang has a tale like this.

In the old times, Zhe Pama created the sky, while Zhe Mima created the earth, and they created man together. Days later, a devil named La Hong did mischief and put a fake sun and moon on the sky, turning the world upside down, plants, water, and lots more. Zhe Pama fought the devil and destroyed it with a kind of virus, shoot off the fake sun and moon, put the world back right back and planted the plants right side up. But the cypress bamboo was not put right. So, the cypress bamboo is like this nowadays. It grows downwards and needs to be planted upside down.

后　记

实在没有想到，《阿昌族动物故事集》会是我这些年在阿昌族中间生活的第一个出版物。这些故事很小却有趣味，应该是那些大人物所不屑的，但是有些老先生会笑呵呵地读。周作人先生晚年以大家之笔，翻译希腊的拟曲、伊索的寓言、路吉阿诺斯对话集，等等，就是看到了这些小故事里的大趣味。

这个动物故事集并非尽善尽美，幸好口头故事从来不追求不刊之论。这些故事是用来讲给人听的，不是写给人看的。而且，每次讲的时候，应该都是讲故事的人的重新创作。

这种过程，我们称为表演，或者学术一点，民间文学艺术表达。表演即创作，写下来的故事，是读不出来灵魂的。

正确的打开方式，应该是在云南德宏州阿昌族的寨子里，和老乡一起围着火塘饮酒唱歌，讲各种离奇的故事，嘲笑一些蠢人。兴之所至，想挖苦或者讥讽某个家伙，甚至编排一个人，就即兴地讲一个故事，故事的主角可以让人马上联想到你所议论的家伙，而且在场的人人心知肚明，从而有一种微恶的口舌快感。

你会的故事越多，你可以动用的素材越丰富，在这样的口舌之辩中，就更有优势，众人随之起哄，大家快乐地伴随对于某个事情和人物的品鉴，喝下烈酒助兴。

我在过去的十年间，多次被阿昌族招待。半生醉酒有三分，二分无端是阿昌。在半醉半醒之中，我答应了杨叶生老师很多事情，有些记得却一直没完成，自己很是抱歉。老人大量，不和我计较，我却总想做一点东西，让他开心。

如果说这篇后记除了感谢杨叶生老师之外，就是希望自己可以多快好省地把阿昌族的传统文化呈现出来，让更多的人知道，有一位杨叶生老师，他和我是忘年之交。

总编：成功

2020 年 4 月 14 日

于碧山居

Postscript

It was quite unexpected that *The Collection of Achang Animal* Stories would be the first publication as a summary of my these years' living among the Achang people. The stories are small but interesting, and may be disdained by the great men, but some old gentlemen would read them with a smile, for example, Mr. Zuoren Zhou, in his later years, translated the Greek mimesis, Aesop's Fables, Lucianos' Dialogues, etc., for the interest in these little stories.

This Collection of Animal Stories is not perfect, but fortunately the oral stories are never mind to be unpublished. These stories are spread in oral form, not in written. And, every time they were told, they had been recreated by the storyteller.

This process is what we call performance, or, more academically, folklore artistic expression. Performance is creation, and a story written down cannot be read for the soul.

The right way to open it would be to drink some wine and sing around a fire pit with your fellow villagers in the Achang people's stronghold in Dehong, Yunnan Province, telling all kinds of bizarre stories and making fun of some stupid people. When the mood strikes, and you want to be sarcastic or ridicule some guy, or even make up a person, you improvise a story, and the protagonist of the story can immediately remind people of the guy you are talking about, and everyone present knows it, thus having a slightly evil tongue pleasure.

The more stories you know, the more material you have at your disposal, the more advantage you have in this kind of verbal debate, and the more people get up in arms, and the more people are happy with the tasting of something or someone, and the more they drink the booze.

Over the past 10 years, I have been entertained many times by the Achang people. If half a lifetime of drunkenness is three parts, and two parts happened in Achang. While half drunk, half awake, I promised

Mr. Yesheng Yang many things, some of which I remembered but never finished, and I was very sorry. The old man is generous and doesn't bother me, but I always want to do something to make him happy.

If this epilogue is not only thankful to Mr. Yesheng Yang, it is because I hope I can present the traditional culture of the Achang people in a quick and easy way, so that more people will know that there is a Mr. Yesheng Yang, who is a cross-generation friend of mine.

Dr. Gong Cheng
In Green Mountain
April 14, 2020